12/97

Pretending
the bed is a raft

Also by Nanci Kincaid

*Crossing Blood*

# Pretending the bed is a raft

stories by Nanci Kincaid

ALGONQUIN BOOKS OF CHAPEL HILL 1997

Published by
ALGONQUIN BOOKS OF CHAPEL HILL
Post Office Box 2225
Chapel Hill, North Carolina 27515-2225

a division of
WORKMAN PUBLISHING
708 Broadway
New York, New York 10003

Grateful acknowledgment is made to the magazines that originally published several of these stories: *Southern Exposure* ("Snakes"), *Story* ("This Is Not the Picture Show"), *Southern Humanities Review* ("Won't Nobody Ever Love You Like Your Daddy Does"), *Doubletake* ("Pretty Please"), *Missouri Review* ("Why Richard Can't"), *The Oxford American* ("Total Recoil"), and *Carolina Quarterly* ("Pretending the Bed Is a Raft").

This is a work of fiction. While, as in all fiction, the literary perceptions and insights are based on experience, all names, characters, places, and incidents are either products of the author's imagination or are used fictitiously. No reference to any real person is intended or should be inferred.

LIBRARY OF CONGRESS CATALOGING-IN-PUBLICATION DATA
Kincaid, Nanci.
    Pretending the bed is a raft : stories / by Nanci Kincaid.
      p.  cm.
      Contents: Snakes—This is not the picture show—Won't nobody ever love you like your daddy does—Pretty please—Just because they've got papers doesn't mean they aren't still dogs—Why Richard can't—Total recoil—Pretending the bed is a raft.
    ISBN 1-56512-177-5 (hardcover)
    I. Title.
PS3561.I4253P7   1997
813'.54—dc21
                                                97-15475
                                                CIP

10  9  8  7  6  5  4  3  2  1
First Edition

*For Lois Swingle Cannon and
in memory of William Henry Pierce*

WITH SINCERE THANKS to Shannon Ravenel and Liz Darhansoff who make the magic happen. To my former students who taught me so much. In memory of Don Hendrie who encouraged this book. To Ali in Africa who gave me such wise counsel. To Leigh in D.C. who read the story "Pretending . . ." to anyone who would listen. And especially to Dick Tomey, who gave me the loveliest gift of all, the time to write.

# CONTENTS

~~~~~~~~~~~~~~~~~~~~~~~~~~~~~~~~~~~~~~~~~~

# SNAKES

~~~~~~~~~~~~~~~~~~~~~~~~~~~~~~~~~~~~~~~~~~~~~~~~~~~~~~~~~~~~~~~~~

*Cherry Lake*

I AM FIVE years old. My brothers, Jimbo and Teddy, are three and one. We are driving with our parents to Cherry Lake to swim. It is summer, so Daddy doesn't have to be Pinetta School principal every single minute; some afternoons he is free to be our father.

We are all dressed in swimsuits. In the back seat my brothers hold inner tubes blown into the shapes of animals, but mine is a simple circle, a pink doughnut shape. The back seat full of inner tubes gives the illusion of more than three children—of a happy occasion like a birthday party with balloons. It is as hot as blazes and twice as hot in the car. It is hot the way only Florida knows how to be, the sun's rays like long, sharp needles piercing our skin, pricking us with heat, the car fender gleaming hot, steam rising from the pavement. Our hair is wet and plastered to our heads, making small, black curls around our ears. The car windows are down, but the breeze is hot breeze. We are happy. Our towels and flip-flops are scattered about the back seat. Jimbo, Teddy, and I take turns hanging our heads out the window, or leaning over the front seat to look at our parents' faces. Are they happy too?

Cherry Lake is not far from Pinetta. The family that lives next door to us goes to Cherry Lake every weekend to fish and swim. My brothers and I stand in the yard and wave good-bye to them on Saturday mornings as they drive off with their picnic basket, pulling their fishing boat on a trailer behind them. But today they stood in the yard and waved to us. They looked surprised as we drove away. It is a Wednesday.

Daddy turns off the highway onto a red dirt road. A sign says CHERRY LAKE 5 MILES. We are nearly there. Palmetto leaves look like green fans on the sides of the road. Daddy is singing. He wants this to be a happy day for us. It cannot be a happy day for Daddy unless it's a happy day for Mother. It cannot be a happy day for Mother unless it's a happy day for us. This is how our family works. So Daddy is trying hard, singing, "The sun so hot I froze to death, Susanna don't you cry." He wants Mother to sing too, and we look at her, hopeful.

"Oh, my God!" she shrieks.

Daddy slams on the brakes, slinging Jimbo, Teddy, and me hard against the front seat. Teddy cries.

Across the road, stretched nearly from side to side, are two huge, fat snakes sunning themselves.

Mother reaches into the back seat for Teddy. "Shhhhh," she says to him, putting her finger to her lips, but looking straight ahead. "Do they have rattlers?" she whispers, her eyes squinted, her voice aimed at Daddy. "Listen. See if you hear their rattlers."

Pinetta is famous for rattlesnakes. Every year they have a rattlesnake roundup, lots of men pouring kerosene down snake holes and smoking the snakes out, catching them in croaker sacks, weighing and measuring them, sending the best snakes to Ross Allen's Snake-Atorium at Silver Springs, where they have the glass-bottom boats. Pinetta takes pride in the size and number of rattlesnakes they have provided Ross Allen. The unremarkable snakes they sell to make hatbands and boots—and some of them they eat. The man who lives next door has been to the rattlesnake roundup. He says rattlesnake meat tastes like frog legs. But we haven't been. Mother doesn't believe in eating snakes. She hates them.

"Don't worry," Daddy says. "I'll run over them."

Mother gasps. Her bare feet spring from the floorboard to the seat. She wraps her arms around her knees. "Okay," she says. "I'm ready. Hurry, hurry."

Jimbo, Teddy, and I lean over the front seat, watching. Daddy accelerates and the car moves forward. We all scream as we drive over the snakes. We imagine them thumping against the underside of the car. We think we feel a bump as we go.

Afterwards Daddy stops the car and we all stare out the rear-view mirror. There lie the snakes, exactly as they were. One snake lifts his head, the other begins to slowly curve himself into a Z.

"They're not dead," Mother says.

"I'll back up," Daddy says.

My brothers and I shriek. We begin jumping up and down in the back seat, slapping each other with our inner tubes. Daddy puts the car in reverse and backs over the snakes. Mother closes her eyes.

Daddy stops the car again to view the damage. The snakes reposition themselves casually, still claiming the center of the road.

"Those snakes must be seven feet long," Daddy says. "I've never seen such big snakes. They don't even feel these tires."

Mother looks at the snakes with horror. They don't seem to understand that we are running over them with a two-ton car. So Daddy tries again. Shifts into drive, then into reverse, running over the snakes without pausing. Jimbo and Teddy and I squeal as we are slung back and forth between the front seat and back seat. Again and again. Now Mother's face is on her knees, her hands covering her head.

"Damn," Daddy says, stopping at last. His hair is drenched. "Can you believe this? Look at that. They won't die."

On the road in front of us are the two snakes, one now belly up and writhing, having been flipped upside down by our car wheels, the other easing its way toward a clump of palmetto leaves on the side of the road.

"Maybe you have to run over their heads," Daddy says.

"They're getting away," I say.

"I hate snakes," Mother says, lifting her head to peer at them, shuddering.

"Run over them again, Daddy," Jimbo says.

There is an unspoken rule in Pinetta. If you come across a poisonous snake you should kill it for the good of the community. Snakes are everywhere. Under the house, in our flower beds, in the weed patch where we play, circled around the leg of a lawn chair in the yard. Jimbo and I have already learned to look for snakes when we walk through the weeds or even when we sit in the shade of the chinaberry tree and draw in the dirt with sticks. We look for snakes every step we take, every game we play, and maybe Teddy does too. Mother has taught us this.

When people in Pinetta kill snakes in their yard they carry them out to the edge of the road and sling them across their mailbox—display them for the neighbors. It's a common sight. Not black snakes and garter snakes. Only rattlesnakes, cottonmouths, and coral snakes. The poisonous ones. Mother says she would not be a mailman in Pinetta for all the money in the world. Many a time a neighbor has hung a dead snake over his mailbox only to find out later that it slithered away as soon as he turned his back. There is no way to count on a snake being dead. Even with their heads chopped off they can still bite you and kill you. So, people in Pinetta take snakes seriously.

"I'm going to have to get out and kill them," Daddy says, opening his car door.

"No," I say.

"Don't," Jimbo shouts.

But Mother was the one. "Don't you dare," she screams, grabbing Daddy's arm, pulling him back in the car.

"I'll get a stick," he says.

"A stick?" Mother looks at him like he's crazy.

"I'll hold their heads down with a stick and grab their necks so they can't bite."

"You're out of your mind," Mother says, still holding Daddy by the arm.

"Then I'll kill them with this." Daddy pushes the car door open and stands on one foot, reaching into the pocket of his swim trunks for his pocketknife. It is the size of a fingernail clipper.

"Jimmy Thornton, get in this car," Mother says. "Please."

Daddy smiles. He begins to open the knife blade.

"Jimmy," Mother says. "Please don't." She grabs his shirt and tries to pull him back into the car. Daddy loves this. He is all smiles. Jimbo and I grab him too, yanking his arm as hard as we can. "Stay in this car where you belong," Mother says. "You're scaring the children." And she wouldn't let go of Daddy's shirt, even when he tried to unpeel the fingers of her fist.

"I'll get the tire jack out of the trunk," he says. "I'll chop them to bits with the jack."

"NO!" we all shouted, frenzied.

"You're bare-legged," Mother says. "If they bit you . . ."

Daddy laughs at Mother. But she will not let go of him. She has stretched his T-shirt completely out of shape trying to pull him into the car. Jimbo and I are pulling too, begging him not to go. And we don't let go until he gets back in the car and slams the door closed.

He pretends a few more times that he will get out and kill those two rattlesnakes once and for all, but each time Mother grabs him and refuses to let him go until he promises not to get out. This makes Daddy happy. He is smiling and laughing.

Meanwhile, the one snake rights itself and then both of them make sedentary exits off the edge of the road through the sand-spurs and into the palmetto thicket.

"Now," Mother says, "we can go."

Daddy grins at her and presses the accelerator. The car moves slowly. "I wish you'd let me kill them," Daddy says.

"Don't be silly," Mother answers. She puts her hand around Daddy's leg as he drives. It is like she is getting a good grip on him in case he should suddenly try to jump from the car and kill some-thing else in the road. He swerves all over the place as he drives.

THAT TRIP TO Cherry Lake I knew my Mother really did love my father. He knew it too, which was why he could barely keep the car on the road.

I don't remember another thing about that day. Not whether we ever got to Cherry Lake. Not whether we enjoyed the buoyancy of our inner tubes, the luxury of staying afloat effortlessly, without having to struggle and kick, without worrying about sinking and drowning. I don't even remember whether we enjoyed the hot dogs we roasted on unraveled coat hangers over an open fire Daddy built of sticks and dry wood.

### The Window

I am ten. We live in Tallahassee now. Daddy has a job with the Florida State Department of Education. He makes more money. We have just moved into our new house. Mother designed it herself and we barely got moved before the babies were born. Mother was expecting, but she didn't know it was twins until thirty minutes before Paula and Pamela were born. Daddy was in Miami. He travels a lot now. So our neighbors drove Mother. She leaked bloody pregnancy juice all over Mr. Covington's car seat. He said, "Don't worry about it," and picked her up and carried her into the emergency room when they got to the hospital. His wife, Ann, carried Mother's overnight bag. They were so nice they made Mother cry. I stayed home and kept Jimbo and Teddy.

We thought we would name the baby Pamela Ann if it was a girl or Wayne Henry if it was a boy. Mother didn't have a name ready when the second baby girl was born. This bothered mother because she likes to be prepared for everything that happens. Paula Lynn didn't get named for three days.

The babies are six months old. Mother doesn't cry as much now. We have a maid, Paris, who comes every day. Before Daddy goes out of town he takes Jimbo, Teddy, and me aside and says, "Now, while I'm gone, the best way to help your mother is to stay out of her way."

Today Teddy is running a fever. He is sleeping in the pine-paneled study, but he wakes up and goes crazy, slapping at the dark knots in the pine. He is shrieking and we all run to check on him. Mother feels his forehead. "You are hot as a firecracker," she says. She hollers for Paris to bring the baby aspirin and a cool rag.

"What's wrong with Teddy?" Jimbo says.

"He has a fever," Mother says.

Teddy continues slapping at the pine knots and crying. He thinks the knots are roaches crawling up the wall. He's trying to kill them. He's beating on the wall with his fist. "Teddy, Teddy . . ." Mother says. "It's okay." She picks him up and kisses him while he struggles in her arms. Then Paris comes with the aspirin and they make Jimbo and me leave the room.

When Teddy falls asleep Mother comes out of the study and walks in to check on the babies in the playpen in the living room. Jimbo and I are watching *Popeye* on TV. Mother bends over and checks the babies' diapers. When she looks up she sees the snake.

"Good heavens!" she says.

Then Jimbo and I notice it too. A snake has crawled up the side of the house and out onto the roll-out window. It is draped half on, half off the glass, sunning itself. Daddy is not home to kill it.

"I'm not studying no snake," Paris says when Mother tries to talk her into flipping it off the window with the broom handle and killing it with the hoe.

We stand in the living room watching the lazy snake, discussing what to do about him. There is nothing but the transparent window screen between him and us. Mother walks over to the window, yelling, "Stay back" to Jimbo and me who want to get a closer look at the snake. She hurriedly winds the squeaky handle, and the window rolls closed. The snake doesn't have time to think what to do. It is clamped almost in half by the closed window. Paris walks over and turns the window handle as hard as she can too, to make sure. It is closed so tight that the snake is pinched in half and dangling. He is caught right in the center of our living room window.

"Now," Mother says. She looks at Jimbo and me. "Don't you touch this window until we're sure he's dead."

The snake hangs in the window for four days. Every time Mother or Paris walk by they try to close the window even tighter. The snake has not moved at all in three days. "His circulation is cut off," Paris says. He is beginning to look dry. The end of his tail is stiff. Jimbo and his friends like to stand outside and throw pinecones at the snake to see if it moves, but it doesn't. We check on him first thing every morning. "Still there," we say.

On the fifth day, Mother is sure he is dead. We watch through the window while she goes outside and pokes at him with the rake. He flops back and forth, lifeless. "Okay," she yells to Paris. "You can unroll the window now." Paris begins the unwinding. "Go slow," Mother shouts.

Pamela and Paula sit in their playpen chewing on rubber clothespins. Jimbo and I watch Mother with admiration. When Paris unwinds the window completely, nothing happens. It is Mother's idea to flip the snake onto the rake somehow and carry it to a little hole Jimbo and his friends dug for the snake to be buried in. It isn't an easy thing. Mother fools with the snake until she gets afraid she will crack the glass in the window with the rake. The dead snake doesn't want to come loose. One last try, and she manages to hook it on the rake prongs and sling it to the ground. Inside the house we all cheer.

But as Mother walks nearer, jabbing lightly at the dead snake, it raises its head. "Lord, God," Paris shrieks. "It ain't dead yet."

"Run, Mother," Jimbo and I scream. She takes a few flimsy whacks at the groggy snake, missing it each time, then she backs up and stares. That snake contracts into a long S and begins to move through the grass. Mother throws the rake at it and runs for the house. We watch the snake slide through the yard, cross the paved road, and go into the woods across the street.

"Good riddance," Paris says.

Mother is afraid to let us play outside until the following day, when Daddy comes home from his trip to Atlanta. He brings everybody presents in his briefcase. Mine is a piggy bank in the shape of a peach. Paula and Pamela get rattles that say WELCOME TO GEORGIA. Mother gets a Whitman's Sampler. And Teddy and Jimbo get rubber snakes. Daddy holds the fake snakes by their necks and slings them out at Jimbo and Teddy, trying to be funny, saying, "Look out."

I laugh, but Jimbo doesn't. He throws his in the kitchen trash can, which hurts Daddy's feelings.

"Hey, Buddy," Daddy says to Jimbo. "What's wrong?"

"If you don't want yours, can I have it?" Teddy asks. He digs through the trash can and gets it out. He holds the two rubber snakes up and puts their heads together like they are kissing at first, then he slaps them together, making them fight.

Daddy looks at Mother and winks.

But all Mother says is, "You are never here when we need you, Jimmy."

### The Flower Bed

I am fourteen. We live in Richmond, Virginia, now. Daddy is manager of a publishing company here and has a fancy office in a tall building on Main Street. He has two secretaries and six sales representatives who work for him. His hair is getting gray.

Mother left six months ago, taking Teddy and Pamela and Paula with her. They went back to Tallahassee, where Mother got a job working in a doctor's office. She fills out insurance forms. I think she will miss the Virginia snow. Last year we had a white Christmas for the first time in our lives. Mother went outside and lay in the snow, she liked it so much. We taught her how to make angels. And Daddy gave everybody ice skates for Christmas. I don't know what good ice skates will do in Talla-hassee.

Jimbo and I want to go live with Mother too, but we never said so when she left and we don't say so now. The two weeks before she left Mother never got dressed. Every day when we came home from school she had on her nightgown. The day she left, yelling for Teddy and the twins to get what they needed and throw it in the car, she was wearing her nightgown and bathrobe and had not combed her hair all day.

"Where are you going?" Jimbo and I asked Mother when we got home from school and saw her loading the station wagon with a mattress and Pamela and Paula's pink Barbie doll suit-cases. "Where are you going?" we screamed.

"You can come if you want to," she said. "Get whatever you want to take with you. But hurry."

Jimbo and I stood watching Mother. Her bedroom slippers flapped as she walked. "Hurry," she told Teddy and the girls, "hurry." It was like somebody nailed me to the floor where I stood. Teddy and Pamela and Paula ran back and forth from their rooms slinging their things into the car, G.I. Joe and all his equipment, Barbie's Fashion Runway and a pillowcase full of her outfits, the report on Zeus Teddy was working on for school, a box of markers with lost lids, two female gerbils in a cage, no socks, no pajamas, no underpants. "I claim the front by the window," Teddy yelled. It was the only thing he said. He sat in the front seat and stared straight ahead waiting for Mother.

"Where are you going? Tell us," Jimbo begged.

"Come with me," Mother said, "both of you."

"We can't," I told her. Daddy will kill himself, I thought, when he comes home and sees this. He will jump off a bridge into the James River. He will die without us—without Mother.

"I'll call you," Mother said, hugging us, crushing us, jabbing her fingernails into our skin. She got in the car and Teddy didn't look at her. He looked straight ahead.

"I love you," she shouted as she backed out of the driveway. We tried to believe her. "I wish you would come with me." Her face was ugly, stretched too tight across her bones, and her hair was wild, she slapped at it, then moved her hand to her mouth and bit it, hard. "I have to go," she said. "I have to."

Pamela and Paula sat in the back of the station wagon on the mattress. They made their Barbie dolls wave good-bye to Jimbo and me in the rear window.

Jimbo and I ran behind the car all the way down the driveway. "It's okay," we said. "Don't cry. The car tag says VIRGINIA IS FOR LOVERS. Our number is LH 4687. I memorized it.

Now some nights Daddy puts a hundred-dollar bill down on the kitchen table. "This is yours," he says to Jimbo and me, "if you will just call your Mother and ask her to come back."

But we won't do it.

Daddy sits in his chair and smokes cigarettes all night. He wants Jimbo and me to tell him what went wrong. He wants us to explain things to him. We try to keep the house neat. It is neater than it ever was when Mother lived here. Nothing is messed up. But Daddy still sits in his chair and says to Jimbo and me, "I've made a lot of mistakes in my life."

Daddy hires Mrs. Foster to stay with use whenever he goes out of town. We hate her.

Daddy spends three nights a week in Washington, D.C. He is publishing something for the government. Mrs. Foster says she bets he has got a woman there. She says, "Your daddy is not the kind to suffer long."

But she never sees him sleeping in his chair. She doesn't see him sit up all night trying to write Mother a letter. He doesn't come into her room in the middle of the night and wake her up saying, "I just had a dream about your mother. Wake up, Bethie. Listen. What do you think this means?"

I tell Daddy that if he doesn't fire Mrs. Foster I will run away. This scares him because he cannot afford to lose anybody else. He says he will think about it. He says maybe Jimbo and I are responsible enough to stay alone.


IT IS TUESDAY. Daddy goes to Washington on Tuesdays. After school Jimbo and I come home and fix bacon sandwiches and watch TV. We sit in the den downstairs with no lights on. We don't talk. We just eat. Mrs. Foster has gone someplace. We're alone. The doorbell rings.

It's the paper boy. He wants his money so I pay him. Then he tells me, "There's a snake in your flower bed." I look where he points. In the pine straw is a long black snake. I yell for Jimbo to come look.

"It's harmless," the paper boy says.

"I know," I tell him.

Jimbo comes out and looks at the snake too. This attention makes the snake decide to climb up the side of the house to get away from us. We watch it crawl up the bricks. "How can he do that?" Jimbo says.

"Don't let him climb up there and get in your attic," the paper boy says. "They like to nest in attics."

I run to get the broom. When I come back the snake is climbing up over the doorway. I swing the broom at him gently, trying to brush him down.

"Give me that," Jimbo says. He swipes at the snake and it falls back into the flower bed.

"He's harmless," the paper boy says, "but where there's one snake, there's two."

The snake begins to wriggle out of the shrubbery and into the clearing in the yard.

"Do you want me to kill it?" Jimbo asks.

"Yes," I say.

"Get the hoe," he tells me. I run to the garage to get it, but can't find it, so I get the shovel.

"That won't do," Jimbo says. "We need the hoe." He goes to the garage to look for it.

I stand watching the snake. It moves slowly. Without thinking what I'm doing I raise the shovel over my head and strike the snake as hard as I can. It bounces. I cannot believe myself. So I deliver another blow. And another one. What amazes me most is that I'm not afraid. It feels good to hit the snake.

"What are you doing?" Jimbo yells.

"It's going to get away," I say, "if you don't hurry."

Jimbo runs over with the hoe and chops at the snake with all his strength. The snake twists and jerks. The impact of the hoe makes marks on the snake's skin, but doesn't cut him open.

"Kill it," I say.

Jimbo beats the snake with the hoe until it is limp and flopping like a piece of soft rope. "Is he dead?" he asks.

We aren't sure. You can never tell about snakes.

"It seems so hateful to only halfway kill him and leave him to die slow," I say. "It's better to kill him completely, all at once."

"Okay," Jimbo says, whacking the snake with the hoe again. I lift the shovel and hit him too, to be sure. We beat him and beat him and beat him. It makes a terrible sound when Jimbo's hoe strikes my shovel. The noise vibrates all the way up our arms and seems to shake our brains.

We keep at it until we are rubber-armed and can't lift our hoe or shovel anymore. "He's dead," I say. "He has to be."

Jimbo reaches down and picks the dead snake up with his bare hands. I can't believe it. He drapes the snake over the hoe and carries it across the street and throws it into the wooded lot over there, shouting as he slings it, making a noise like a Tarzan yell, only worse. I stand in the yard and wait for him. When he turns to walk back home I look at his boy face. I love Jimbo.

WHEN WE GET inside the house the phone is ringing. It's Mother. She knows Daddy is in Washington on Tuesdays, Wednesdays, and Thursdays.

"Hello," I say. "We're fine," I say. "How are you?"

She says she and the little children miss us. She says she loves us.

"Jimbo just killed his first snake," I say. "He beat him to death with a hoe."

Mother gets quiet. "Let me talk to him," she says.

But Jimbo won't. He turns on the TV and listens while Douglas Edwards reads the world news. "He can't come now," I say.

"I'm proud of him," Mother says. "Tell him that."

"I will," I say. And we hang up.

I walk outside and sit on the front steps. The shovel and hoe lay slung across the walk. We should put them away before Daddy comes home. I like to sit outside in the late afternoon and breathe cool air. I like to watch the cars drive by our house, sometimes with their headlights on, fathers heading home from work, sleeping as they drive, and short-haired mothers with back seats full of neighborhood children, delivering them home from baseball practice and piano lessons, stopping to let them out, their good-byes echoing up and down the street, like the saddest music in the world.

## THIS IS NOT THE PICTURE SHOW

~~~~~~~~~~~~~~~~~~~~~~~~~~~~~~~~~~~~~~~~~~~~~~~~~~~

ME AND PAT Lee go to town every Saturday. It is a social responsibility. Only the country kids don't go because they have to feed chickens and stuff, which we think is the saddest of circumstances.

When we get to town we buy five-cent bags of boiled peanuts first thing from crazy old men who sit on the sidewalk, some with their legs cut off and their pants all folded and pinned in strange arrangements, some blind who take all day making change, feeling each coin, counting out loud, and some who are okay on the outside, but crazy in the head the way they sing songs without words, or make a bunch of kissing noises when they see me and Pat Lee walking up.

"Shut up, you stupid old men," Pat Lee mumbles.

Mother says these crazy old men are left over from the war or else let out of Chattahoochee Mental Hospital. She drops us off at the park right where they sit and says, "It's pitiful. You two be nice to those pitiful men." And every Saturday of our lives we pay one of them our nickel and get ourselves little warm, wet bags of juicy boiled peanuts.

Then we roam through all the stores in downtown Tallahassee looking at merchandise. Actually we are looking for other junior-high people who are also roaming. When there are seven or eight of us, maybe more, we go from place to place, trying out 45 records in the listening booths at the Sammy Seminole Music Store. Sometimes we connect the dots on the acoustical tiles to see what they come out to be. (Once we fit thirteen people in one listening booth, just for the heck of it, and played Chubby Checker records on 78 speed, which is the funniest thing you ever heard.) Then we eat French fries at the Rexall and write messages on the tabletops without getting caught. Me and Pat Lee make up initials, like T.B. + V.D., and paint them on in fingernail polish, knowing other people will come along and try to figure out who it is. The waitress has never mentioned a thing about it.

After that everybody rides the elevator at Mendelson's Department Store. We hold the buttons down and just keep going up and down—not stopping to let any other people on. We do that ten or fifteen times and then we go to the cosmetics counter and spray each other with sample cologne. Until, finally, it is time for the picture show and we all walk down the street to the State Theater.

Now the State Theater does a good business. They could show black-and-white slides of "How to Care for Houseplants" and we would line up to see it. It is fifty-five cents to get in and for another nickel you can get an all-day Sugar Daddy on a stick, which we always do. If you are ever going to have any experience with boys this is the place to get started with it, which makes me nervous, although I manage to be as suave as the next girl about it. I have to be. Because of Pat Lee and all.

It comes natural to her, driving boys crazy. She does it by acting rotten to them. She does it by being mad at them all the time, or bored to death or aggravated with them for some reason they never can figure out. I've seen boys get in a fistfight outside the State Theater over who was going to sit by Pat Lee, only to have her get mad and refuse to sit by either one of them. I've seen her sit by Bobby Castle all the way through an Elvis Presley movie with her arms crossed, pouting, not saying a word to him. But he still bought her buttered popcorn, an Orange Crush, and a box of Milk Duds. And when the movie was over he asked her if he could sit by her again the next Saturday, tried to make her promise, and she walked right out of the theater without even looking at him. That night he called and asked her to go steady. It's like that all the time.

Pat Lee says the reason the boys don't like me as much is because I'm too nice to them. She says I make her sick going around smiling and being thoughtful. She says no boy will ever take me seriously until I stop it. I try to tell her that I don't mean to smile this much, it's just that my face seems to automatically go into a smile, even when it's in a resting state. Pat Lee says it's disgusting and is trying to get me to start saying "shit," and "tits," and "screw" and a bunch of other words that will wipe this smile off my face. She gives up on me all the time. She says deep down boys cannot stand a nice girl. "You're prettier than me," she says, "but I'm a whole lot more popular than you. So I guess it balances out." I can only hope she's right.

Pat Lee's popularity got started in the sixth grade when she was the fastest runner in the school—and nobody could beat her and almost every boy in the class tried. She did not throw like a girl either, which made boys go crazy over her. They would line up at P.E. just to watch Pat Lee pitch a baseball. And she could hit home runs and shoot baskets from midcourt and do a backward flip off the high dive in her red bathing suit. Everything boys respect. Then all that admiration just mushroomed into this other thing. And Pat Lee is the most popular girl at Augusta Raa Junior High School. She gets elected to everything she tries out for. And I kind of like it because I get the spillover from her popularity. If a boy can't sit by Pat Lee, then he wants to sit by me, since I'm her best friend. I don't have to go to much trouble over it. I even let Proctor James sit by me, despite the fact he never washes his hair. He sat by Pat Lee first, but she got up and moved, making all the rest of the boys laugh at him. The next thing I know I felt so sorry for Proctor I was smiling at him.

"You're hopeless," Pat Lee said to me. "I swear to God, you're hopeless."

"He's sort of nice," I lied.

The only boy Pat Lee thinks is nice is Tony Kelly, and that's only because Tony is almost as mean as she is. And he is a country boy too—not like the rest of the boys at the picture show on Saturday in their penny loafers. His brother lets him out in front of the State Theater in a souped-up green truck—which anybody else would be embarrassed over—and Tony neither speaks nor looks at a single person in the picture-show line. And he wears boots, which are not in style at all. And sometimes lights up a cigarette like he has a perfect right to do it. He does not fit in in any way, and doesn't even try to, and so people can't help but stare at him and wonder just what he thinks he's doing. I stare at him myself.

The first Saturday he showed up at the State Theater all the regular junior-high people got quiet and looked at him. He didn't care. And before you know it Pat Lee walked over to Tony—the whole civilized junior-high population gawking—and said, "Hey, Tony. You here by yourself?"

"You see anybody with me?" he answered.

"Do you want to sit with me and Connie Jean?" (I was hoping he'd say no. Pat Lee had already promised to sit with Bobby Castle.)

"It depends," Tony said.

"On what?" Pat Lee said, not smiling exactly, but sort of playing with her hair.

"I don't like a bunch of talking when I go to the picture show," Tony said. "I'm not paying my money to listen to girls talk."

Pat Lee didn't get mad, and she sat beside him that Saturday and every Saturday since. Nobody can understand it. She has let Tony kiss her three times. Once at *Lover Come Back,* once at *Where the Boys Are,* and once at *How the West Was Won.* I was sitting right next to her every time. When they start that, it makes my hands sweat. And worse than that, it gives the town boys the same idea. They think Pat Lee is practically a goddess now that they know she will kiss in front of everybody.

And Tony, even though his hair is too long, he doesn't peg his blue jeans, and just wears white T-shirts all the time, nobody makes fun of him. If he walks into the State Theater late and Pat Lee is sitting with Bobby Castle because she thinks Tony is not coming, all Tony does is walk down the aisle with his hands in his pockets, not even looking for Pat Lee, just maybe chewing a toothpick, and he goes and sits by himself and waits. And when Pat Lee sees him she hurries over there, saying, "I'm sorry. I didn't know you were coming." And Tony says, "Shhhhh, I'm trying to watch the show."

At school Tony will not speak to Pat Lee. He's in the dumb classes for one thing, the vocational boys, woodshop and all, and so he just minds his business at school. If you ask me he's failed a grade or two. It wouldn't surprise me if he'd been to reform school. Pat Lee laughs and says I'm crazy when I tell her that. "You're jealous," she says.

"I don't have anything against boys from reform school," I say.

"You don't have anything against anybody," she says. "That's what's wrong with you."

Pat Lee tried to save Tony a seat at lunch once, but he said, "No," and took his tray and sat at a table all by himself.

She got so mad she stormed over there saying, "I don't see what gives you the right to go around acting like you're better than everybody."

"Go sit with your friends," he said.

I thought for a minute Pat Lee was going to cry. But she said, "Are you coming to the show Saturday?"

"Maybe," he said.

ME AND PAT Lee usually get to the State Theater early but we are probably the only two people in junior high who don't always get to see the show. Our mothers worry about appropriateness.

On this occasion, when *Gypsy* was the Saturday show, our mothers said, "I can't think of a reason in this world why two young girls need to see a movie about a stripper!" So we had to just stand outside the State Theater and watch everybody else go in. We could just see all the junior-high people sitting in the first rows, and it made us miserable to think we wouldn't be sitting there too. It made Pat Lee even more miserable than me, for fear

Tony would come and she would miss seeing him, or worse, that some other girl might try to sit next to him and he might let her do it.

We stood on the sidewalk sucking soft-boiled peanut hulls, then spitting them on the ground. We stood there until every single person had filed inside and there was no one left but the two of us.

"I guess he's not coming," Pat Lee said.

"Who?"

"Who do you think?" Pat Lee said, shoving me down the street. "Let's go to Woolworth's."

Woolworth's is two doors down from the State Theater and they have this banana-split special. They have a bunch of balloons taped to the wall above the counter. The customer picks out one and the waitress pops it and gets a piece of paper out of it with the price of the banana split on it. Sometimes a person gets a banana split for a penny, but most of them are thirty-nine cents.

We sat in the booth up by the window, chose our balloons, and sat waiting for our thirty-nine-cent banana splits. We have never paid less for a banana split and don't know anybody else who has, but we believe in the game and remain hopeful.

Pat Lee is one of the few people I can talk to in a serious way. We've been best friends since third grade, and over the years we developed a radar. For example, I knew, without Pat Lee saying so, that she was watching every vehicle that went down Monroe Street, hoping to see that souped-up green truck.

"You still looking for Tony?" I said.

"Nope."

"You know why he makes you so miserable?" I said. "It's because he's as mean as you are."

"At least I don't hold hands with Proctor James."

"I DID NOT HOLD HANDS."

"You sat by him."

"ONCE."

"You are so nice you make me sick," Pat Lee said. "I bet you grow up and marry one of those boiled-peanut men."

"Shut up," I said.

"This is the real world out here," she said. "This is not the picture shows."

The waitress brought our banana splits just then, two beauties with beehives of whipped cream on top and red cherries sliding, leaving pink trails. She set them down carefully, trickles of chocolate dripping down the sides of the glass boats. As soon as the waitress left, Pat Lee said, "Yours is bigger than mine."

"Good," I said.

"But your banana has a rotten spot on it," she said, scooping a mound of vanilla ice cream into her mouth, "so it balances out."

Pat Lee is my best friend. But she can make me hate myself sometimes. It's because she's honest, I think, which Mother says never has been in style and never will be. Mother says that honest is another word for rude. Like if somebody is fat Pat Lee'd say, "Lord, that girl wears her groceries, don't she?" When Beth was too flat-chested to undress in P.E., Pat Lee said, "Listen, Beth, get you a bra and stick some toilet paper in it. That's what Caroline does." Caroline was mad at Pat Lee for a long time, but Pat Lee didn't care. You'd think her mother had never mentioned the first word about good manners.

I don't hold this against Pat Lee, though, because she is Catholic and I feel like that has something to do with it. My mother says that Catholics just do what the Pope says and they don't have to think for themselves, so I always keep that in mind.

We paid the waitress and began wandering up and down the dime-store aisles. We know the store by heart, same as we know every store in Tallahassee.

Neither one of us really felt like hanging around uptown by ourselves, knowing the rest of the world was in the dark theater watching some grown woman undress to music.

"Today's been a bomb," Pat Lee said. I was surprised at Pat Lee sounding ready to go home. She usually loves to stay in town more than anybody. "Let's walk over to Penney's," she said. "I'll call Mother to come get us."

J. C. Penney's is between Woolworth's and the State Theater. It is the official place where people call their mothers. I gave Pat Lee a dime to call with, since it was her mother coming to get us. Things are always confused at her house. They have eight kids. It usually takes a lot of time just to get the right person to the phone and then her mother has to remember where everybody is or should be. It is mass confusion, which is why Pat Lee doesn't like to be home much and doesn't like people to come over to her house and see what a mess it always is. One of her brothers has drawn a Sears truck on the living room wall with an orange crayon. Now they have to paint the whole room. There is a lot of crying going on over there and screen doors slamming. That's why Pat Lee prefers to come to my house. It's quiet. My mother spends her life cleaning everything up. After saying *okay* about ten times, Pat Lee hangs up.

"Mother said she has to take Missy to tumbling class at the armory and then she'll come get us. She said to meet her in front of Penney's because her hair is rolled up and no way is she going to trek through the Penney's store looking for us with her hair rolled up."

"Okay," I said. "Let's go upstairs and look at the clothes a few minutes."

They had a whole rack of new bathing suits set up. We both headed straight for it. "Are you getting a two-piece this year?" I asked Pat Lee.

"Probably. If you don't, boys think there is something the matter with your body." She held up a little butterfly bikini. "Shoot, I bet seeing me in this could straighten Tony Kelly out. Bet this could turn the boy nice."

Pat Lee was greatly exaggerating her powers—believe me—and besides, her mother would never in a million years let her buy a bathing suit like that.

"Good gosh," she said, pulling out a second bathing suit and waving it around in my face, "they must have chased a nigger down for this one."

"Shhhhh," I said on instinct. I looked around us, afraid some colored person would hear her. Afraid some colored person would get mad and give us that quiet look I hate more than anything. There were a couple of salesladies at the counter deep in whispered conversation, and some girl older than us carrying a dress into the fitting room. "Be quiet," I said.

"This bathing suit is even too tacky for a nigger," Pat Lee said.

And then I saw her—an old lady, who came walking from between some racks of raincoats. Pat Lee was analyzing bathing suits a mile a minute by this time.

"Hey," she said, "get a load of this."

But I was watching the old lady. She moved slow, like she was dragging something, watching her feet every step she took. On her head was a black straw hat—the kind old ladies wear—and she carried a big tourist pocketbook with gaudy flowers all over it and the word FLORIDA stitched in red straw across it. She stood at a counter of madras shorts and as slow as Christmas picked up one thing, put it down, picked up another thing, put it down.

She had on a pair of old Hush Puppies—somebody probably gave them to her—and dark stockings with a run in both legs, showing streaks of skin. And her dress, it probably used to fit somebody just right, some other woman a long time ago. There was a hole in the elbow of her sweater, which it was too hot to be wearing anyway. But it wasn't her clothes that got my attention, it was her face and the fact that I couldn't see it. She was stooped over and her eyes stayed down. Just that black hat on her head shining out like a blank face with the eyes, nose, and mouth erased off of it.

I guess she'd picked up and put down every item on that table. Her back was to me now. And with unnatural stillness she moved her arms at such a slant, like she was reaching for something, and that pocketbook of hers came open. Then quick—so quick I wasn't sure I saw it—she stuffed a handful of shorts into her pocketbook, and it was closed again.

I got hot all over. There I was watching her and the old lady stole something. My heart was beating away, like it was me doing it, stealing. I couldn't move my eyes away from her.

"What's with you?" Pat Lee was hollering. "Hey, what are you staring at?"

"Shhhhhh," I said.

Pat Lee turned to see what I was looking at. When she did, the old lady was sticking some more clothes in her pocketbook and Pat Lee saw her too.

By this time I knew it was the real thing. But Pat Lee felt that same shock like I had. "Good gosh," she whispered. "Look at that. She's stealing. Would you look?"

I couldn't quit looking.

The old lady should have felt us staring at her. Our eyes should have seemed like little bullets going into her back.

"We've got to tell somebody," Pat Lee said. "Come on. Let's

tell somebody. She can't come in here and clean the place out. Shoot, a granny like that."

"Wait a minute," I said, grabbing Pat Lee's arm so she couldn't go. "She's old."

"Have you gone crazy?"

"Look at that pitiful dress," I said. "It's so pitiful." It crossed my mind that this old woman might be a sister to some of those old men that sat in the park selling peanuts. She might be crazy like some of them and have spent her whole life at the Chattahoochee Mental Hospital and just got released into Tallahassee without having any idea how to act in the regular world.

"What's right is right," Pat Lee said. "You know that."

But I didn't. There is nothing in this world that I am sure of. "What do you think they'll do to her if we tell?" I said.

The old lady didn't look anything like my two grandmothers. Both of them are fat. I knew for a fact it had never crossed either of their minds to steal anything.

"It's our duty to turn in people when they start robbing the place blind," Pat Lee said, her eyes contracting into slits. "You wait here if you're chicken. Just keep your eye on her. Don't let her get away."

I tried to act regular watching the old lady shuffling around the counters. Maybe it was a terrible thing—shoplifting. It probably was, since they send people to jail over it. What if everybody did like me and watched old ladies steal shorts from the junior-teen department? J. C. Penney's would have to close down in no time.

If she could be a colored woman stealing, I thought, well, then it would make sense and I wouldn't be so worried about it, because everybody knows colored people have certain reasons for what they do. But everybody also knows there is no good reason for any decent white woman to be stealing. My mother has explained it to me, that any wrong thing a colored person does, it is because we make them do it. Us. White people. But I don't know where she gets that. Because I can honestly say that I, myself, have never made a colored person do anything.

I stared at the old woman like she was stark naked, scooting around in nothing but those Hush Puppies. It was not my fault she was poor, was it? It was not my fault she had that wrinkled face and wore that pitiful dress and had got caught stealing like any other thief in the world. Why did it seem like my fault?

I thought about running up and telling her to empty that tacky pocketbook before the police came. I thought about screaming for her to run like heck. I could have warned her. But then I bet Pat Lee would say it was her duty to turn *me* in as an accomplice. I would have to go to court, which would break my daddy's heart and make him divorce Mother for the crazy ideas she put in my head. I would be sent off to reform school, where I would turn into one of those vocational girls who takes cosmetology classes, dyes her hair, and wears bras as pointy as two sharp arrows. They would probably kill me at reform school because I am so nice. They would tie me up in ropes and leave me on a cold cement floor, or else beat me with slats of lumber until I went unconscious. And they would scream, "You are too nice. This is what you get for being so nice!"

The old woman floated like a small gray ghost around the store. I am afraid of any person who will not let you see her face. It seemed forever before Pat Lee came back. Some man wearing a name tag came with her. And it was done.

"Let's get out of here," Pat Lee said. "We've done our part. Besides, Mother's probably waiting out front."

The man with the name tag walked over to the old lady, taking hold of her arm. "You'll have to come with me," he said.

A great puff of air seemed to go out of the woman, shriveling her the last bit, but she was obedient and allowed herself to be led away, shuffling along beside the stern, closed-faced J. C. Penney's man, clutching her Florida bag with its cheerful straw flowers. "I need to call my grandson," she said.

"Yes, ma'am," the man said with strange politeness. Maybe, like me, he believed this was all somehow his fault.

"Hurry," Pat Lee said. "Mother will kill us if she has to get out of the car with her hair rolled up."

The man slowly escorted the little bent-over robber downstairs to call the police. They passed in front of Pat Lee and me, the old lady watching her step, staring at those hand-me-down Hush Puppies.

We passed a full-length mirror in the men's department before we reached the front door. Pat Lee stopped a minute and looked at herself, pushing her hair up with her fingers, puffing it.

"Do you think I ought to start ratting my hair more?" she said. "I bet it would make me look older. I bet Tony would like it."

"You're too nice to Tony," I said. "Every other boy you treat hateful and they all like you because of it, but Tony you're nice to and he hardly pays you any attention at all. You make a fool of yourself acting so nice."

"You don't understand," Pat Lee said, fluffing her hair again, twirling around, holding her arms out at her sides. "It's love," she said, grinning. "It balances things out."

Pat Lee's mother was late. We stood on the sidewalk for twenty minutes, waiting, before Pat Lee finally went back into Penney's and called her mother again. "She forgot us," Pat Lee said, coming back out of the store, "but Missy says she's on her way now."

Just as Pat Lee finished speaking, like the timing in a movie, that green pickup truck Pat Lee had hoped to see all day came lurching to a halt in front of J. C. Penney's. Tony sprang out of the front seat, leaving the door hanging open, and hurried toward us. His brother sat in the driver's seat and kept the motor running. He was smoking a cigarette and had a tattoo on his arm. He looked like one of those men my mother sees and says, "The army would be the best thing in the world for him." He did not look like Tony, who has not got so sour yet, and who walked past us full of intent, his boots clicking across the sidewalk.

"Hey, Tony," Pat Lee said, but he seemed unable to hear her or see her, either one. He seemed only able to see what was directly in front of him and he walked straight ahead toward it, whatever it was, right past us, and through J. C. Penney's swinging doors.

"He didn't even speak," Pat Lee said.

"He didn't see you," I told her.

Just then Pat Lee's mother pulled up in her station wagon and began blowing the horn, as if we were likely to miss seeing her otherwise. She had brush rollers with pink spikes stabbed through them all over her head and a scarf tied uselessly over them. She was happy because she and Pat Lee's daddy had been invited to dinner at Tallahassee Country Club that very night. They were not members but socialized with lots of people who were. Her fingernails were painted red and she had the radio going, playing Glenn Miller's "Little Brown Jug." Three of Pat Lee's younger sisters were huddled in the very back of the station wagon with a scattered set of paper dolls to keep them busy. One of her brothers sat in the front seat with his arm hanging out the window. "Hurry up," he said. Me and Pat Lee got in the back seat after scooting over some bags of groceries that were piled in our way.

"You won't believe what we saw," Pat Lee said to her mother. "There was this really old woman in Penney's teen department . . ."

As Pat Lee was speaking, the old woman appeared, walking out of Penney's, shuffling slowly, looking down. She was holding onto her grandson, who walked patiently beside her, extending his crooked arm so that she could brace herself walking.

"Isn't she pitiful," Pat Lee's mother said, noticing the old woman and craning her neck to look harder. "So pitiful."

The pair moved across the sidewalk to the waiting green truck and its open door, she in her Hush Puppies and he in his pointed cowboy boots and white T-shirt.

Tony gently helped his grandmother into the truck. It didn't seem to matter to him whether she was crazy, or a criminal, or wearing raggedy mismatched clothes. It didn't seem to matter to him that she had just got caught stealing, and it would probably say so in the *Tallahassee Democrat* the next day. It wouldn't matter to him if she was just released from Chattahoochee yesterday or due to check in tomorrow. He spoke softly to her and when she was seated in the truck cab he slid in beside her and slammed the door closed.

The green truck jerked out into traffic right in front of us, and when it did Tony caught sight of Pat Lee, her face watching him from the back seat of the station wagon. His elbow was jutted out the window, and keeping his arm still he lifted his hand in recognition as he passed, raising a couple of stiff fingers and nodding slightly.

Pat Lee fell back against the seat, silently. And I understood it. Why Tony makes her smile like that. Why she loves him more than any other boy in Tallahassee. For a minute there, I loved him myself.

# WON'T NOBODY EVER LOVE
# YOU LIKE YOUR DADDY DOES

~~~~~~~~~~~~~~~~~~~~~~~~~~~~~~~~~~~~~~~~~~~~~~~~~~

*I*

TAMMY'S MOTHER, NORMA June, was a good-looking woman. Everything she did was like a good-looking woman, smile, laugh, tease with her teeth in a way that can't be explained. Smoke the friendliest cigarettes anybody ever saw, when she wanted to. And fix up. Serious fix up, with a drawer full of Merle Norman creams, lipsticks, eyelash curlers, and powder she patted every place there was.

The women in the neighborhood could not decide what it was about Norma June that nudged her across the line to the good-looking side. Suzanne, her best friend, said it was her hair. She had good hair. Dark brown with shine to it and natural curl and a Falstaff beer rinse once a week. Some of the women said it was her eyes, green like they were, with eyelashes like lips. Eyes that sort of puckered up and kissed out at things. She had good skin too, and talked about Merle Norman like it was a relationship.

"Merle Norman has done wonders for me," Norma June said. "I swear by him, I do. Wouldn't be the woman I am without him." Of course, Norma June thought Merle Norman was a man, since she never heard of any woman named Merle. Besides, as far as Norma June was concerned that's what men were for— to make a woman feel beautiful.

Norma June was married to Barton, who was big. A photo of him in his army suit sat on a table in the living room. It was the way he looked when she married him—big, and soft-faced. Now he was just big. Filled up whole doorways being big. And Norma June had sense enough to know some things when she married Barton, like it would take a big man to be married to a good-looking woman like her.

Every Friday and Saturday night Barton took Norma June out someplace. He'd been doing it since before they even got married, taking her out to show her off. Sometimes they got a colored woman to come stay with their kids, Tammy and Tony. But as the kids got older more and more they just let the TV babysit. That and their big yellow dog, Sunset, who Norma June had named.

On Friday and Saturday nights Norma June locked herself in the bathroom and communed with Merle Norman while Barton

made Tammy and Tony some mayonnaise and banana sandwiches. Sometimes he made hamburgers, or fish sticks. Got the
kids some supper and glasses of milk in greasy Tupperware cups
and then got himself dressed to go, and sat on the sofa in front of
the TV, where Tammy and Tony were sprawled out on the floor,
and Sunset was too. Sunset with that tail scraping back and forth
on the hardwood floor, back and forth, back and forth, like one
of those things that hangs down inside a clock and ticks back and
forth.

When Norma June was finally ready she unlocked the bathroom door and entered the room like a vision. Norma June liked
to wear black. She said it was her best color—black—and had
lots of dresses she proved it in on Friday and Saturday nights. She
waltzed into the room and made Barton smile as she turned
around slowly in her beaded cocktail dress and little black pat-
ent slippers. Norma June twirled right up in front of the TV so
everybody in the room had to notice. Tony said, "You look
pretty, Mama." And Tammy said, "You sure do. Will you save me
that dress till I grow up, Mama?"

"I sure will, Sugar Cube," Norma June said. "When you grow
up then you and your Mama will share this dress, all right?" And
Tammy reached out to hug her Mama, trying hard not to smudge
her powder or smash her hair. Norma June blew a little kiss on
her fingers and tapped it on Tammy's cheek. "There you go, little Sugar," she said.

Once Norma June was dressed to go it was not unusual for

Barton to wait another half hour, him and the kids, while his wife went next door to the neighbors' houses, just two or three of them, to show how good she was looking since people were always interested in that. Her friends were, the ladies in the neighborhood.

Norma June tapped on the back door and tiptoed into the kitchen. "Yahoooo," she sang out, casual, like some woman coming by to borrow a cup of cornmeal. "Yahoooo, Suzanne, you home? It's me, Norma June. Wanted to show you my dress." And Suzanne barreled out from the back of the house in her pedal pushers and her husband's shirt she was using for a maternity top and her flapping house shoes.

"Norma June Hartell. Let me look at you." And Norma June started twirling again.

"Good gracious," Suzanne said, "if Cinderella went around in black dresses she could be you. Come in here, Jack," she yelled to her husband, who was already on his way into the kitchen. "Come get a look at Norma June." Jack came in with his glasses on and a newspaper in his hand. He looked at Norma June still twirling around the kitchen, and nodded his head up and down.

"Doesn't she look pretty?" Suzanne said.

Jack just kept nodding. Then one of the babies started crying and Suzanne hurried to the back of the house, leaving Jack to see Norma June out. Norma June tiptoed out the kitchen door, smiling, and tossing her beer-flavored hair in Jack's face as he stood holding the screen door open for her. "Wish me a good time," she said.

"Have a good time."

"Oh, you know I will." Norma June started out across the yard. "Tell Suzanne I'll call her tomorrow and tell her everything." Jack nodded some more, and watched Norma June make her way to the next house, where LuAnn and Blakney Steadman lived.

And when Norma June finally went back home to Barton, heavily dosed with admiration, she smiled and was almost mushy over him. She gave him little kisses and smoothed his hair with her hands, and straightened his tie that didn't need straightening.

When Barton and Norma June said good night to Tammy and Tony, Norma June patted Sunset, saying, "Be a good dog, Sunset, and look after the kids." And Barton bent over and whispered something in Tony's ear that made him smile and nod yes, then Barton said to Tammy, "Come here and give your daddy a kiss, little girl." And Tammy put her arms around Barton's neck and gave him a loud kiss you could hear. "That's a good girl." Barton said. "Your daddy loves you, Baby." Then Barton and Norma June got in the car and drove off to the American Legion Hall or the Elks Club or any place that had some music and liquor, and low lights or bright lights—either one. Any place where the people had sense enough to appreciate a good-looking woman.

Sometime after midnight Barton and Norma June came back home just a little bit drunk, or maybe more than just a little bit. Norma June took off her high heels and tried to tiptoe through the living room and back to the bathroom in her stocking feet so as not to wake up little Tammy and Tony, who were sprawled out

on the floor still in front of a jabbering TV with every light in the
house on. The two of them, with the spread off Tammy's bed
pulled over them, asleep on the hardwood floor, and Sunset
there with them, her back-and-forth tail going. Norma June
stepped lightly over the children, careful, in her unsteady, giddy,
I-could-have-danced-all-night condition.

And Barton came in, stumbling behind her, with his shoes like
those a big man wears. Shoes that sort of shake a floor. He
reached down and scooped up the children, one in each arm
with the bedspread draped between them half on and half off. He
carried them both back to their beds, flopped them down so
gently they never even woke up, and he arranged their arms and
legs some way that looked comfortable and pulled a sheet over
them, and pulled the hair back out of Tammy's eyes. He did this
with his whiskey breath and loud shoes. Aimed to place a wet
kiss on each of their small faces, but was off target and kissed
their hair, or an ear. Then Barton turned off the lights and went
to bed himself, and waited on Norma June to take her makeup
off and put her cream on. He always waited as long as he could.

## II

When Tammy was almost twelve and Tony was nine, Barton
lost his job at the meat-packing plant, but got another one within
two weeks, traveling for Golden Flake Potato Chips. Had his
own territory. They paid him by the mile too. But it meant being

gone most of the week, just coming home weekends, or sometimes being gone most of a weekend, too. But Barton made up for that. Made good money. Brought presents home from time to time. And in the summer when he could he took Tony with him on the road. A man and his boy doing a job for Golden Flake Potato Chips.

"Tammy," Barton would say when he left, "you take care of your mama now. Hear me. And me and Tony will bring you something. What you want? A 45 record?"

"Doesn't matter," Tammy said.

"Look after your mama now. Help her when you can."

When Norma June lost her Friday and Saturday nights to the potato chip company she took it all right. Better than anyone expected. Because, good-looking woman that she was, she had friends. She had Suzanne and Jack next door, her best friends since the day they moved in. Suzanne that she whispered with at the line, hanging clothes, that she loaned a dress to every New Year's Eve until Suzanne gained all those extra pounds and couldn't fit into anything. And when Suzanne miscarried her second baby it was Norma June that lay down in the bed beside her and patted her back until she finally fell off to sleep. Patted her back like a soft little heartbeat—and it helped some.

And Jack was a friend too, a quiet one, that didn't say much, but did not complain when Norma June gave Suzanne ammonia permanents in the kitchen which took four hours altogether and left supper so uncooked that Jack finally took the kids to Tastee-

Freez for chili dogs. It was Jack that came up to Norma June's with a flashlight that time she heard funny noises at three o'clock in the morning and Barton was off in Moultrie. And it was Jack that went on and cut the grass for Norma June when her yard got to looking like a neighborhood embarrassment with Barton gone too much to keep it right. Jack would just go on and cut both yards as long as he was cutting.

Sometimes that first summer, when Barton and Tony were out on the road, Norma June got sort of dressed up and took Tammy out to a restaurant for supper. They would go someplace that had good fried fish and served half-price liquor to un-escorted ladies. More than once they got their whole dinner free. Good-looking Norma June and her daughter, Tammy, who wasn't but twelve but already showed signs of promise. Had those kissing eyes like her mama. Soon as she was old enough to put some mascara on those eyes there wouldn't be no stopping the girl. People said that sometimes.

Once a man at the bar had walked right over to their table and picked up the check out from under a water glass, and when Norma June protested, he said, "Now, honey, don't argue. You and your sister here enjoy your supper. Y'all sure helped me enjoy mine."

And so Friday and Saturday nights kept on for Norma June, with or without Barton. From time to time when Barton came home, pulled up in the driveway like company coming, he'd get out with presents. Something foolish and useless for the kids that they always liked. Maybe nothing but some stalks of sugarcane to rot their teeth and make them sick. Maybe a record for the hi-fi, "Purple People Eater" or something. Once some coconuts with seashell feet, and crazy faces carved out and painted, and big earrings in each ear. But he brought Norma June presents in wrapped-up boxes, and she never unwrapped them so Tammy and Tony could see. She just took those presents and kissed Barton's face. Him eyeing her like he never saw her before in his life, his own wife, eyeing her while she goes to the back of the house and closes the door to open her presents.

"What you and your mama been up to?" Barton asked.

"Nothing," Tammy always said.

"Well, good," he said, grabbing Tammy up and swinging her around in the air, same as he did when she was six, same as he'd probably do when she was twenty-six. "Your daddy is glad to be home," he said. "Ain't no place like home. Ain't that right, Tony?"

"Naw," Tony said. "There's too many girls in this house when you're gone, Daddy. They run me crazy. I wish I could keep on going with you."

"You got to look after your mama and sister some," Barton said. "Women need a man to look after them, keep 'em out of trouble. That's your job when I'm gone."

"Tammy ain't no woman," Tony said.

"Well, she's gon' be. Soon as me and you blink our eyes a few more times your sister is gon' be a grown woman. Gon' be as pretty as her mama, and worry me to death like your mama did her daddy. 'Cause Tammy is just like your mama. Gets more that way by the minute. You can see that, can't you, son?"

"No," Tony said.

Barton smiled at his daughter—the same smile he gave Norma June sometimes—so Tammy recognized it, and knew to go to the refrigerator and get the man a cold beer when he smiled at her like that.

### III

When Tammy was almost fourteen she started baby-sitting Jack and Suzanne's kids after school since Suzanne had taken a job at the hospital working the three-to-eleven shift. Tammy watched the kids until Jack came home, usually around seven, sometimes later. She got the kids their dinner, and Jack too. Sometimes he came home looking so tired and worn out that Tammy just stayed on and gave the kids their baths, got them into pajamas, and read them off to sleep. She was glad to do it.

Sometimes Jack sat at the kitchen table and smoked cigarettes and listened to Tammy read out loud. Other times he got a beer and sat in the living room with the newspaper, or watched TV until Tammy went in and said, "Jack, will you turn that thing down some. Your kids never will get to sleep with that thing blaring." She said that to a grown man and her not fourteen yet. And she liked it how Jack mumbled, "Sorry," and went over and turned the TV down. Sometimes turned it off. And put on the hi-fi, and played Johnny Mathis or something nice like that that kids could go to sleep to.

And in her head Tammy started this game. It was about Jack and the kids. She played like it was her house, the kids were her kids, and Jack was her husband. Played it every day after school while she baby-sat. And when Jack came in from work she had him a place set, and some supper ready. Tomato soup maybe. Or tuna fish. And she kept things picked up, and mothered Jack's children like they were hers, because in the game they were.

When the kids got to sleep she straightened the kitchen and put the dishes away. Jack smoked cigarettes and sometimes took off his glasses. Tammy emptied his ashtray and talked to him sweet as she could because she was practicing up for how it would be when things came true and she really did have her own house and kids and husband. Maybe a husband sort of like Jack, but probably not. Jack was sort of handsome, had hair so black it was almost blue (Suzanne always said he was part crow—the bird, not the Indian), and with his glasses off he had such nice eyes that Tammy could hardly look at him without being embarrassed. But he always seemed quiet and serious, like he was worried.

Sometimes she felt sorry for his kids. Half the time he forgot to pick up his little girls and swing them around when he came home from work. More than once Tammy had had to remind him to kiss them good night—until she had just started bringing them in to him, the girls fresh out of the tub with their curly wet hair and Cinderella shorty pajamas, and Jackie, the baby, in his diaper with a bottle hanging from between his teeth and mismatched socks on his feet. She carried them in to Jack and sat them on his lap—all four of them—every night so he could love them and wrestle with them a few minutes and throw them up in the air and catch them. But it never happened just that way, mostly he sat quietly while the children swarmed over him, giggling, fussing, like so many pink puppies. Jackie always yanking at Jack's glasses, sometimes pulling them off. And when Jack said, in a too-loud voice, "Bedtime," then Tammy marched the children to their bedrooms and tucked them in, while Jack reached for a Kleenex tissue and began to clean his glasses.

So even though Jack was a good practice husband—fine for the make-believe life she was trying out every afternoon after school—she thought that when the time actually came she would probably marry somebody more like Barton, big like that, and real nice. A man who would lie on his back on the floor, put his big feet on the soft bellies of her children, and fly them up in the air making airplane noises. A husband who brought secret wrapped-up presents and called her "Babydoll," like her daddy did her mama.

One night when the kids were asleep and the dishes washed and put up, Tammy was getting ready to walk across the yard home, when Jack said to her, "Tammy, you know how to dance?"

"A little bit," she said. "I can fast dance good. You want me to show you how to fast dance?"

"Naw," Jack said. "Fast dancing is for kids. I just felt like dancing, slow dancing, thought maybe you knew how."

"Sort of," she said.

"Come over here and I'll show you."

And she did. And he did. Taught her to slow dance like Arthur Murray would. Official like that. And as the nights passed they might dance some. Wait till the kids were asleep good and dance and laugh a little bit. Tammy even tried to show Jack the fast dances she knew. He watched her with interest, tried it himself just barely, just enough to amuse Tammy and make her giggle. Tammy thought it got to be the best part of the night.

The first night they danced with the lights off it was because Jack said it was more relaxing that way. They danced at least five slow songs. Jack held her so close she thought it was like they were a couple of candles—like the music lit their heads, and was melting them together. It was the nicest smell. She closed her eyes because there was nothing to look at. And Jack brushed the hair away from her face sometimes, and kissed her neck. And whispered her name with his lips that were a little bit wet against her ear. Tammy thought this meant he loved her.

But Norma June didn't like it. Tammy coming home at ten or eleven o'clock every night, not getting her homework done, not helping around her own house anymore. Norma June said it would not do, and she put an end to it. Wanted Tammy to come home the minute Jack walked into the house. She said Jack was a grown man and could look after himself. Tammy could not protest much because she was too embarrassed to explain about the game.

And Norma June watched to see too, watched for Jack's car in the carport, and as soon as she saw it she would stand on the porch and wait for Tammy. It made Tammy so nervous. Hurrying like that. Jack knowing she's got to hurry because her mama is standing there, waiting, for the world to see, with her hands on her hips. And sometimes Jack gave Tammy a friendly swat on the bottom real easy, as she was hurrying out the door. Swatted her that playful way and called her "Mama's girl."

WHEN SCHOOL FINALLY let out for that year Tammy quit babysitting because Suzanne hired a colored lady to come and keep the kids and cook supper. And because it was summer again, then Tony went off with Barton every chance he got, going places on business and staying in motels. Barton still saying to Tammy every time he left, "Look after your mama, now."

It was mid-July when Suzanne went to visit her people in Louisiana. Took all the kids with her. Jack couldn't get off work to go, said just the peace and quiet of them being gone would be vacation enough for him, and he grinned saying it. His car left the driveway about eight o'clock every morning, came back around seven just like always. A couple of times Tammy saw him go inside carrying a sack from the barbecue place, for his supper, she guessed. Probably gon' sit over in that house and eat his barbecue with the relaxing lights off and the hi-fi going. Tammy could picture it.

Norma June missed Suzanne, but LuAnn and Blakney were good about inviting her to do this and that thing with them, play some cards, drive down to Madison and bet the dogs, fry some fish in the yard. One night they invited her to go see some kind of Rock Hudson–Doris Day double feature at the drive-in, and she wanted to go in the worst way. She wanted Tammy to call up a friend and spend the night out, so she would not have to worry about her at home all alone. But Tammy didn't want to call anybody. She like being alone, having the whole house to herself. She promised to lock the doors. So Norma June finally said okay, and then went in the bathroom and spent one full hour, maybe longer, getting ready, rattling things in her Merle Norman drawer, singing to herself the whole time.

"Sugar Cube, you be good," Norma June said as she left. "Keep the door locked and go to sleep when you want to. I'll let myself in with the key." And she left to walk down to LuAnn's. She looked mighty good to be going off to sit in a dark parked car where nobody would even see her, but that was Norma June's way.

It was hot July when every minute seems like it is leading up to something. When everything you do is wet. It is too hot to sleep. The window fan moans twenty-four hours a day. Tammy watched some TV. Two different boys called her on the phone, but she didn't talk long because it was too hot and she didn't like the boys much anyway. She ate almost a whole bag of Golden Flake potato chips, but it didn't help that July feeling.

Around ten o'clock Tammy took a bath. Sat in the tub of

water to cool off. Shaved her legs. Got out and put lotion all over and baby powder on top of that. Then just for something to do she got into Norma June's Merle Norman drawer—got out all the tubes and compacts and polishes and put them on to see what she could turn into. Put on mascara and blue stuff on her eyelids. Did all the magic things to her own face that she had been watching her Mama do for years and years. Was almost good at it, and she liked what she saw when she was done. Liked the way those little tubes of lipstick and pink lotions and powders gave her five more years than she'd really earned, five years she could wash away when she wanted to. Tammy brushed her hair, pinned up one side of it with a hair clip, and let the other side hang loose and free. She felt good. As she was admiring her face, talking to herself in the mirror, the phone rang. She blew a kiss at her reflection and went to answer it.

"How's the sweetest girl this side of New Orleans?"

"I'm fine, Daddy."

"You ain't just fine, little girl, you're as fine as fine can be, you know that, don't you? And I'm still your best boy, ain't I?"

Tammy recognized all the energy Barton put into his talking —it was how he did when he was half-drunk. Talk loud, like he was singing.

"You miss me?"

"Yes."

"Where's your mama? Put your mama on the phone."

"She's not here."

"Shit." Barton said. "Where is she?"

"Don't say shit, Daddy. She's gone to the show. Her and LuAnn and Blakney."

"I'll be dog," he said. "Here I am a lonely man calling his wife and she's gone off to the picture show. I'll be dog."

"What are you doing, Daddy?"

"Thinking about your mama's ass."

"Daddy," Tammy said, "Don't talk like that. Don't say ass. Me and Mama don't like it when you talk like that. Mama says it isn't you talking, it's Jim Beam."

"Well, she ought to know. Do you miss me, Baby?"

"Yes, Daddy. I already told you yes."

"You always gon' be your daddy's girl, ain't you? Won't nobody ever love you like your daddy does."

"I know. I'll tell Mama you called."

"You do that, little Babydoll."

"I'm not gon' tell her what you said though."

Barton laughed.

Tammy hung up the phone. Her daddy got that way every once in a while. Sort of nasty drunk. Sort of lonely for Norma June and he called late at night, woke up the whole house, saying he just wanted to hear Norma June's voice. Sometimes she acted glad he called. She acted sweet over it. But sometimes she got mad, said she just as soon sleep as talk to Mr. Jim Beam himself. Sometimes she got on the phone and fussed, said why in this world didn't he use the good sense God gave him?

But Tammy didn't think of all that now. She looked at herself in the mirror again. If she ever wanted to she could be one pretty girl, she knew it was the truth. Might be as pretty as her mama. She got bold and went into Norma June's bedroom closet and tried on her best dresses. Some of those black dresses, none of which fit exactly, but some came close. One looked as good as Tammy thought a dress could ever look on her. She zipped it up and pulled the belt as tight as it would go. She twirled. She looked in the mirror from a hundred different angles. Smiling. Tossing her head. She sat in a chair and looked in the mirror. Crossed and uncrossed her legs. Then she lay on the bed and posed like all the glamour women she had ever seen in magazines. She was practically in love with herself over her good looks. Merle Norman magic. It seemed terrible to waste looking this good. Someone needed to see her to make it true.

Jack's car was in the carport, the porch light was on, and maybe one on in the living room. He might still be up. It was only eleven-thirty. Tammy would twirl herself down to Jack's house. Go to the kitchen door and knock. He would open the door with a cigarette in his mouth. He would stare at her in disbelief—he would have to put his glasses on—"Tammy?" he would say. "Is that you?"

But what would she say to him? She needed to think of something to say before she went. She did not want to have to think on her feet, not in Norma June's high-heeled shoes.

"Jack," she would say, "I came to dance one slow dance. Mama is off at a show. So we can dance one slow dance." Tammy decided the lights would probably be off already, the music going already, and she would let Jack kiss her again if he wanted to. And when he whispered her name the third time, it would be time for her to leave. She had it planned. Third whisper and she would say, "Well, I better go now," and she would run across the yard, fading into the night like a dream. She would vanish like Cinderella and leave Jack standing there in his sockfeet like a stupefied prince. Then she would wash her face, hang up Norma June's dress, and go straight to bed.

When Tammy got almost to Jack's kitchen door she noticed Sunset behind her in the darkness, slow walking. Doing the old-age limp. But it was too late to go back and put her in the house. Tammy's shoes tapped across the driveway in what she thought was a too-loud manner, so she began to tiptoe instead.

She heard music before she even got to the door. That much was good. And the house was almost completely dark, just a pale rim of light around the edge of the window. Seemed like Sunset was making a lot of noise in the flower bed, but Tammy managed to be quiet, and to position herself just right to see inside.

Jack was there. She saw his cigarette burning in an ashtray, and his glasses on the table. It was perfect. Everything was perfect. It was just exactly like she imagined, except for one thing, one detail. Her mama, Norma June.

There was Jack, the pretend husband—his shirt unbuttoned, the hair on his chest as black as a fluttering crow's wing—hold-

ing Norma June in his arms like all it was was hugging and there
was no music at all. And Norma June's hair was a mess. Her good
hair all loose and tangled. Jack and her mama blurred together,
the two of them so tangled, so blended it made Tammy rub her
eyes and smear blue stuff up the sides of her face. "Oh God," she
thought, feeling as if she had been dropped from an airplane, fast
falling through the night air.

If Jack was whispering her mama's name Tammy could not
hear it. Her ears rang so loud she couldn't hear anything. Ringing
in her ears like if an ambulance drives up to your very own house
with the siren going. She was sure she was not screaming. It was
just some siren going off. Sunset's tail flapping away faster and
faster, like a hand slapping an invisible face.

Tammy tried to run home, but her feet wouldn't run, they
only stumbled right out of both high-heeled shoes, left lying
somewhere in the yard. She went in the side door and locked it,
unpeeling Norma June's dress as she went. She was hurrying the
way a person about to vomit hurries. She ran to the bathroom
and began to wash her face, makeup smeared everywhere. Black
and blue streaks across her face, red smears from her lips to her
nose. "Shit," she said. "Shit. Shit. Shit." She kept rubbing, but
it seemed like she was just rearranging the mess—not getting
it off.

She put soap on a washcloth and rubbed again, her skin
pinkened until it was the same color as the lids on the Merle
Norman cosmetics she had left sitting out on the counter by the

sink. She swung at them suddenly, her washcloth like a whip, and knocked them across the room, where they bounced against the tile, crashed into the tub, and rolled across the floor under her feet, making a noise like Tony's little toy trucks. She scrubbed harder, but those extra five years—they did not wash off.

She threw the towel on the floor and went into her mama's bedroom and began rummaging through the bedside table looking for the telephone book and the mimeographed paper that was kept folded inside it, Barton's travel schedule. It was so Norma June could find him if she needed him, in case of an emergency. Tammy found it in the G pages, G for Golden, and unfolded it. July. She thought she might vomit. July 17. Valdosta. Friendly Motor Lodge. It was almost twelve o'clock. Barton would be asleep. It was a long-distance call. Practically midnight. Tammy dialed. An irritated clerk put the call through. Tammy's stomach churned.

"What the hell?" Barton's angry voice said.

"Daddy?"

"Who the hell is this?"

"It's me, Daddy."

"Good Lord, what time is it? What's wrong? What's happened?"

"I just wanted to talk to you, Daddy. That's all."

"What's wrong?"

"Nothing."

"Where's your mama?"

Tammy dug her fingernails into her flesh, gripping hard, to stop the falling. "She's gone to the movie, Daddy. I told you that. She's on her way home right now. She's just a couple minutes late."

"You okay?" Barton asked. "You sure you're okay? I swear to God you scared the hell out of me."

"I just miss you, Daddy. That's all."

"You like to give me a heart attack."

"I love you."

"I love you too, Baby. You know that, don't you?"

"Yes, Daddy."

"You go on and get to bed now. I'll be home in a couple of days, and I'll bring you something nice."

Tammy hung up the phone and searched through the bedside table for a pen and wrote on the back of Barton's travel schedule, "Mama, your husband called you tonight." She left the note sitting on the pillow on Norma June's side.

It was after midnight now. Outside she could hear Sunset whining. In her hurry to get home Tammy had locked the old dog out because she was too slow in coming, so now she would have to listen to her whimper, scratch at the door, and whine. All night long she would have to listen.

It was not until she lay in her own bed with the door to her room locked that Tammy began to cry. It was her belly. And it was her face. She rubbed her skin and it burned where she touched it. She put her pillow over her head, and the cotton pillowcase felt soothing. She kept it that way for a long time hoping the darkness would help. But no matter how dark it got, Tammy could still see.

SHE WAS NOT asleep when Norma June's key rattled the door, unlocking it. She heard the sound of Sunset's nails scratching across the hardwood floor, heard Norma June whispering to the dog, "Shhhhh," as she tiptoed down the hall to her bedroom. Tammy got out of bed and followed her.

She watched Norma June take off her shoes, sling them across the room. Norma June picked up the note on the pillow. Her lips moved as she read it. She crushed the note until it was the size of a clenched fist and jammed it into the bedside drawer. Then she walked to the dresser looking at herself closely in the mirror, running her fingers around the edges of her eyes.

"So," Tammy said. "How was the movie?"

Startled, Norma June twirled around and looked at Tammy as if she were reading something written in small letters across the girl. "It was fine." She turned away and began undressing.

Tammy watched as her mother unbuttoned her blouse, took it off, and hung it up in the closet. She unhooked her bra and held her arms out in front of her to let it slide off. She undressed gracefully, as though she were performing before a live audience, as though she were saying to the world, "See, this is the beautiful way to take off a bra and fold it and put it in a drawer." Norma June's immodesty infuriated Tammy, the sight and sway of her mother's breasts as she slid a nightgown over her head, the way she slid out of her panties, left them lying on the top of the dresser, picked up a brush and began brushing her tangled hair. All of this as though Tammy were not watching her—but everyone else in the world was.

"I saw you with Jack tonight," Tammy said, her voice slipping out from under her. "You were letting him . . ." She stopped and closed her eyes. "I saw what you were doing."

Norma June's half-brushed hair, full of electricity, stood out wildly on the side of her head. She was pale. Tammy pictured Jack kissing away all the makeup her mother had carefully applied. It was as though he had licked her clean, eaten off the outer layer of perfect skin.

"You're too young to understand," Norma June said.

"I'm telling Suzanne."

Norma June looked at Tammy with naked eyes.

"Can't you at least say you're sorry?" Tammy demanded.

"I'm not sorry."

Tammy shook her head to keep the words from settling. "I hate you."

"No you don't," Norma June whispered.

"At least I know right from wrong, which is more than you can say."

Norma June laughed. Her voice was a saw slicing the night in two, half for Tammy, half for herself. Her jaggedness frightened Tammy, cutting her off, making her drop like a limb from a tall tree, she fell and fell at the sound of it. "Stop laughing," she ordered.

"Oh, God," Norma June said, throwing her head back, running her fingers through her hair, one side electric, the other side knotted. "Listen to me. Try to understand this." She paused and looked at Tammy as though she was searching for something with no hope of finding it. "Jack and I see this line between us, do-not-cross-or-else, okay? We see it. But the line comes to life, Tammy, and circles us, wraps its tail around us. And before you know it we're all tangled up—and the crazy thing is—"

"You're crazy."

"When I was fourteen I had good and bad memorized too, but things change places, Tammy. That's what they don't tell you."

"Poor Daddy."

"Damn it, everything is not about your daddy."

"I'm telling him."

"You want to play God?" Norma June said. "Fine." She went to the bedside table, dug out the travel schedule, picked up the telephone, dialed the number, and handed Tammy the receiver. "Play God," she ordered. "Tell your daddy everything. Don't leave anything out."

Tammy put the receiver to her ear. It was ringing. "Jack doesn't love you. If you hadn't been there he would have—"

"What?" Norma June asked. "Danced with you?"

Tammy pressed the receiver hard against her face with both

hands. Tears filled her eyes as if someone had said on your mark, get set. She was going to cry like a stupid little girl.

Norma June stepped close and put her arms around Tammy, a melting, not an embrace. A moment of fear passed from Norma June into Tammy, then gave way to dizziness. Tammy was unsure which of them was the mother and which one the daughter—for a moment they were both the same woman standing in different points in time.

Tammy thought of Norma June in Jack's arms, legs entwined, arms wrapping, wrapping, wrapping, the way Jack was kissing her and kissing her. "I thought Jack liked me," she said.

Norma June rocked Tammy back and forth the way she must have done—although Tammy couldn't remember it—when Tammy was a little girl. "My sweet Sugar Cube," she whispered. "Of course he likes you."

Tammy swayed with Norma June, still holding the telephone receiver in her hand.

"Jack would be crazy not to like you. But, Sugar, he's old enough to be your daddy."

"Friendly Motor Lodge," the telephone voice said. "Hello?"

"And a girl doesn't need but one daddy." Norma June took Tammy's face in her hands, wiping the tears with her thumbs.

Tammy pictured Barton asleep in his underpants, his big, white body sprawled across the motel bed.

"Anybody there?" the voice kept saying. "Hello? Hello?"

## PRETTY PLEASE

~~~~~~~~~~~~~~~~~~~~~~~~~~~~~~~~~~~~~~~~~~~~~~~~~~~~~~

I LOOKED FOR proof all my life and found enough evidence
to mount a fairly decent defense, you know, in case I was ever
taken to court and made to prove anything to the world. But I
wanted better than fairly decent. I wanted to know for certain
that if Daddy was called down to the police station he could pick
me out of a lineup of daughters. "That one," he would point at
me, "is my daughter, Lee." After which I would break down and
confess everything.

He read to me when I was young, the little engine that said,
*IthinkIcan, IthinkIcan, IthinkIcan,* and all about princesses who
were awakened by kisses and swept away into the *happyeverafter*
by handsome princes. Even about the beautiful girl, no older

than I was, who could kiss frogs and turn them into perfectly decent men.

He drove me to Sunday school too. Rose had to be at church unnaturally early, and Daddy was left with the task of constructing my ponytail out of the thin wisps of my uncooperative hair. He went at it like he was building a bookcase. He tied my sashes into limp, heartbreaking bows that I was glad I couldn't see. He paid for me to go to Baptist church camp every summer without complaining and always gave me five dollars to waste while I was there. He never spanked me or yelled at me or punished me for anything. He said *I love you too* when I confessed my love for him—but it always felt like I was saying *thank you* and he was using the same words to say *you're welcome*.

Most nights we ate suppers where Rose and I chatted and laughed and tried to haul Daddy into the conversational boat we struggled to keep afloat. But he always sat in his chair like a big fish at the end of our witty and enticing lines and no matter how we tugged he never budged. I think now that if we had ever managed to pull him into the boat—which was the family, our tiny two-woman family—he would have sunk it altogether by just the pure weight of his unhappiness. Even now sometimes I think of my father as the fish that got away. A whale of a fish. I think of myself and Rose as wasted bait he wouldn't take, like we were a couple of frantic pink worms twisting ourselves into voluntary knots around the heart-shaped hook we hoped he'd swallow. But we never even seemed to tempt him.

The less sure I was that Daddy loved me, the more desperate I was to love him well, so well that maybe he could not help reciprocating, even against his will. So I set out to do my part and his part too. The more he withheld, the more I gave. I was determined not only to put in my half of the love, but also to put in his half for him since he was so ill-equipped to do it himself. I guess this was when I began my career as would-be savior. If I couldn't be Daddy's Jesus, then I would be his Virgin Mary.

I thanked God regularly that I was pretty enough. It was the thing I believed Daddy valued most about me. He rarely told me I was pretty but he looked at me sometimes in a way that let me think he thought so. I recognized the look because it was the same one I had seen him aim at women who walked past him on the street, after which he mumbled to me, "She was attractive."

Also, whenever I invited girlfriends to our house and introduced them to Daddy, his only comment would come later, after they had gone home, when he remarked on whether or not they were pretty—or just exactly how pretty they were. He might say, "Frances Delmar is a pretty girl." This meant he liked Frances Delmar. Or "I'm sure Margaret is a nice girl, but she's not a bit pretty." This meant he did not like Margaret. It was a code between us that I understood perfectly. He was never rude to any friend I invited home. He was always a perfect gentleman.

When we were in high school and Frances Delmar started wearing tight skirts, Daddy said, "Frances Delmar isn't as pretty as she used to be." This meant Frances Delmar was getting trashy. I lived in terror of the day Daddy might decide I was no longer pretty. To ward it off I spent a great amount of time learning to *fix up*. Late afternoons Rose said to me, "Lee, honey, you might want to fix up a little. Your daddy will be home soon." Rose herself was in a constant fixed-up state, which loomed before me like a living example.

I tried not to let Daddy see me with curlers in my hair or unshaved legs or blemished skin. It felt too much like failing a test—like letting him down when he was depending on me. The happiest moments of my life were when Daddy, after surveying the girls in my Sunday school class, or at a spend-the-night party, or dressed for a dance, would lean over and whisper, "You're as pretty as any girl here." It never mattered that it wasn't true.

Even Lilly, our maid, was not immune. When I rode with Daddy to take her home in the afternoon, he always overwatched her walk up to the porch and fumble to unlock her door. He watched the way her hips shifted as she put one foot in front of the other, the way she braced the screen door with her elbow while she rummaged through her purse searching for her house key. "Lilly is a fine-looking woman, isn't she?" he said. "I don't care if she is colored."

I hoped Daddy didn't go around saying this to just anybody, especially not Lilly, who I knew for a fact didn't allow white men to look her over. The nicest thing she had ever said about Daddy was that he wasn't "bad as some them white mens." And once she'd said, "Your daddy is right harmless." I wanted her to keep thinking so. She would not like him sitting out in a hot car with the motor running, paying her compliments behind her back. I didn't like it either.

Daddy worked leisurely hours as the manager of an insurance company that his father, my grandfather, had owned. Now it belonged to Daddy. He was not a salesman. He was an owner-manager. This was a relief to Rose and me since we could never imagine Daddy persuading anyone to buy anything and were glad our livelihood didn't depend on such a thing. Daddy's life was less about persuading than about never being persuaded. From as early as I can remember, even though I loved Daddy desperately, I made a decision to choose a husband very different from him. One who would not be so much work. I wanted to marry a happy man. A man who just came happy—automatically, all by himself—so it wouldn't be my job to make him that way.

Maybe from the stories Daddy had read me I got the idea that I should be Daddy's princess and Rose should be his queen. I became fixed on making this happen. Rose and I did our parts. For one thing, we both pretended Daddy was the king of the house. We did this two ways, by pretending that he owned the house and everything in it, including us, but at the same time we treated him like a special guest just stopping in from time to time to eat a good meal and watch a little TV. We didn't disturb him if we could avoid it. We didn't upset him. We didn't make demands. We only, on occasion, made polite requests. He almost always obliged. If he was a king didn't that make Rose a queen?

Didn't that make me a princess? But Daddy wouldn't pretend back. Not that part about us.

Balls were what Daddy loved most. He played golf every weekend year-round and lots of afternoons after work, too. This is the main thing I ever heard Daddy and Rose argue about—the hours he spent on the golf course—especially when he missed church to do it. "Maybe the golf course is my church," he said once. "Maybe golf is my religion, Rose. Did that ever occur to you?"

She didn't mind the money he spent joining country clubs or the money he bet on golf games. I don't even think she minded the drinking and the way he slurred his words when he got home—but she did mind sitting alone in the pew on Sunday morning. She minded being asked where Bennett was when he ought to be in church and having to think up something believable to say to people who had no intention of believing her and were asking just to be hateful.

Daddy had season tickets to BU football games and followed high school football too. He acted like this was his real job, he was getting paid to do it, and his salary was already up into the millions. It's the only thing I know for sure he was ever serious about. He put a basketball hoop in our driveway and on rare occasions he shot baskets with me until after dark—unless Jett was around. Jett was Lilly's son. Daddy hired him to do our yard work. He liked Jett because Jett was a real good football player at his black high school. "Put that rake down, son,"

Daddy would say. "Let's me and you shoot some hoops. A little one-on-one." He made me sit in the grass and watch the two of them go at it. "Run get us a cold drink, Lee," he'd say, staggering around the driveway after the ball, panting, sweating, gasping for breath, making me think of a firm inner tube going soft, a leak someplace inside him that nobody could find, nobody could patch.

Jett beat Daddy every time. As much as Daddy hated losing, I knew he fully expected to lose and that was why he liked to play with Jett—because Jett would see to it that Daddy lost. And Daddy wanted that proven to him over and over again, that it was his destiny to lose. But it was clear he loved Jett for winning. Daddy had natural admiration for winners. It was like he was born admiring men who were better with balls than he was— even if that man happened to be black and more of a kid than a man. I guess that maybe those were the only moments Daddy ever came close to questioning white supremacy—but I'm not really sure.

Daddy watched football and golf and basketball and anything else ballish he could find on TV, but not boxing or horse races or car races because there were no balls involved in those. He tried to identify with the guys holding the trophy, accepting the check, or putting on the green blazer at the eighteenth hole at the Masters. These were his people—he wished. Winners. Their lives should have been his life. But something had gone wrong. He longed for the winner's circle and loved without reservation the men who lived winning lives, who mumbled their humble thanks into microphones on our television set.

This put Rose and me at a terrible disadvantage. We felt we needed to win something too, in order to become real in Daddy's eyes. In order to show up at all on the TV screen, where Daddy watched for almost anything worthwhile in this life to happen. Rose was trying to win God's love. But me—what could I win?

More than once I went to sleep secretly wishing I was a son. Imagining myself as some sort of home-run hitter or some speed demon who could dodge the onslaught of defensive linemen whose job it was to destroy me. I could get my picture in the paper the way Jett did, and then Daddy could read about me and know that I was worthy.

But the truth was Daddy had little respect for female athletes because he rarely found them pretty. There were a couple of professional women golfers who were the exception. He would call Rose and me into the den and point them out to us on TV. "Look at this," he'd say, "she's pretty good-looking for a lady golfer." The women always had blond hair and suntans. I had blond hair and a suntan, too, but there was nothing in me that longed to hit a ball, or kick one, or catch one, or throw one, or do anything at all to one. I wasn't inclined toward balls. I was too much like Rose. This was the whole trouble. And in my heart I blamed Rose for this.

It would be wrong to say that I ever gave up on wanting

Daddy to love and adore me, like I imagined surely all other fathers did their daughters, but I made a deal with God that I would forgo being loved by Daddy in that essential way. I promised God that I didn't mind if Daddy didn't love me the way he should, as long as he would love Rose the way he should. I am dead serious when I say I would have much preferred that Daddy love her than me. If he loved Rose enough, then I thought I could live off the scraps of their love. It would be enough.

But I never saw him hug or kiss her or laugh at anything funny she said. He was not mean though. He did what she said to do for the most part, pick up Lilly in the mornings, get the Christmas decorations out of the attic, change the lightbulb in the bathroom, hose down the driveway. He didn't argue with her much. It was just that he obeyed so silently that he became ghostly to us. In dramatic moments I think my childhood was haunted by his ghostliness. It was my constant longing to be good enough, pretty enough, to bring him to life, to puff a breath into him that would resuscitate him or to speak words that would jump-start his heart—to somehow prove to both of us that he was real and alive. Not to wake him up with a kiss exactly, like all those stories he read me, but just to wake him up somehow. I got the idea at a very young age that love was an earned thing and I must work very very hard to deserve it.

"FRIDAY IS MARCH fifth," I said. "Don't forget." I was always the one to remind Daddy of Rose's birthday.

"Here." He'd hand me a Pizitz credit card to buy her a gift from him. "You've got a better idea what she likes than I do." This was sad but true.

I picked out extravagant gifts for Rose: perfume sets, lacy slips and panties, silky nightgowns, add-a-pearl necklaces, and once a black satin French push-up bra, trying to fool my mother into thinking my father loved her. I wrote sweet cards and signed them *Love, Bennett*. I wanted her to believe that Daddy had searched the world over to find just the right gift, something romantic that would say to her all the things I feared he never said himself. Early on I took it to be my job to trick them into loving each other.

I WAS IN junior high when the rumors first made their way to me. Girlfriends who heard their parents talking, whose fathers played golf with my father, whose mothers mentioned other women's names in sentences with my father's name. They delivered those sentences to me at school the next day—my friends. These sentences were hand-delivered like ropes to hang myself with, but I refused. I accepted each length of rope like it was really a ribbon for my hair, like it was something lovely and I was glad to have it.

"Don't pay attention to them," Frances Delmar said. "Your daddy is handsome. Lots of women probably flirt with him. That's all. Boy, I'd love it if anybody ever flirted with my daddy." We laughed because Frances Delmar's daddy was totally bald and totally fat. But he also loved her perfectly average-looking mother like crazy and I thought he worshiped the ground Frances Delmar walked on.

ONE DAY AFTER school, the Tri-Hi-Y went to visit the Alabama Home for the Incurables, an old folks' home, mostly, that also had some deformed and insane children in it, too, who had no place else to go. There was a picture of Jesus hanging above every bed. It was our job to write letters for the bedridden patients as a service project. The Home for the Incurables seemed sort of like a pleasant prison. The people were strapped to their beds because they were loved, not because they were being punished. The nurse told us that. The patients wanted us to write letters to their family members, whom I secretly believed would never write them back.

I accidentally wandered into the room of a girl my age. I wished immediately that I hadn't. She seemed so glad to see me that I felt instant guilt about having never been there before. It's like when you walk into a place for the first time in your life and you know at once that you should have come sooner and oftener, but you also know you will never come back for the rest of your life if you can help it—you know all this in an ugly instant. The girl had a soup-bowl haircut and too many teeth to fit into her smile. She had a disease where her muscles had minds of their own—and maybe her mind had muscles of its own, too—but the two were not connected. She didn't get to be still for even one second of her life. Everything was always jerking, jerking, even when she slept, I guessed.

"Hi," I said, trying to act like she was a girl from school, like I had known her all my life. I was casual. I got out my stationery and fountain pen. "Would you like me to write a letter for you?"

She smiled, nodded, then began the task of saying the word "yes." She made "yes" into the longest one-syllable word in the history of the world. I thought I would grow old and die before she finished the word.

"Who do you want me to write to?" I sat in the metal folding chair beside the door with the stationery in my lap and my pen poised. I tried to smile at her but it was hard because I was beginning to hate myself, my luckiness, my ability to sit still, which I had never appreciated, and the fact that I knew better than anyone that I didn't deserve to be lucky and probably God knew it by now and wished he could do things over and make me the girl in the bed and the girl in the bed me.

"Annnnnnnnnnnnnnnnnnnnnnna."

"You want me to write to Anna?"

She shook her head in big negative circles and tapped her finger on her chest.

"You don't want me to write to Anna?"

She pounded her finger harder against her rib cage. "Meeeeee."

"You're Anna? Oh," I said, "your name is Anna." My God, I hadn't even asked her her name. Everybody has a name.

"I'm Lee."

She smiled at me and nodded yes.

"So who do you want me to write to?" I scooted my chair closer so I could hear her and touch the bed if I decided to. Touch her leg maybe.

"Cheeeeeeeeese sauccccccccccce."

"Cheese sauce?" This was not going to work. She wasn't making sense. It seemed like I wasn't making sense either. We didn't have any shared words to volley back and forth. It was like we were trying to play verbal tennis only she had a bowling ball and I had a baseball bat and the net between us was too high anyway. "What? You want some cheese sauce?"

She shook her head in hard circles, then pointed to the wall above her head.

"Oh," I said. "Jesus. You want to write to Jesus?"

She nodded.

"Okay," I said. "Jesus it is." I scrawled across the stationery, "Dear Sweet Jesus."

AT FIVE O'CLOCK the members of the Tri-Hi-Y gathered in front of the Home for the Incurables to wait for the mothers who would carpool us home. "Look, Lee. There's your daddy." Frances Delmar pointed to my father's car as it passed in front of us. We waved but he didn't see us.

THAT NIGHT AT dinner I talked about Anna just enough to say she had written a letter to Jesus, which I had mailed for her care of Rose Carraway, my mother, at First Baptist Church.

"How lovely," Rose said. Rose was big on getting messages to and from Jesus.

I also recited bits of a letter an old man had written to his daughter who lived in Ohio. Lord only knows if she'd ever write him back. Rose listened and shook her head. "There's nothing like family," she said. "Family is everything."

Then, like a fool, I said, "We saw you this afternoon, Daddy, when you drove by the Alabama Home for the Incurables."

"Not me," Daddy said.

Of course it was him. He drove his car like he lived his life— as if the thing he was doing was never really the thing he was doing because in his head he was always off someplace better doing something better. Like that. He looked handsome though. I was proud of the somber-faced man who drove by us, dis- tracted, in his shiny black Buick.

"But it was you," I insisted. "I saw you myself. We all saw you."

"Then you must be seeing things," Daddy said, his eyes steady and blue. "The Home for the Incurables is all the way across town and I didn't leave the office all day. Came straight home after work."

Right before my eyes he was transforming into the ghost that haunted our house. "It wasn't me," he said flatly.

So I accepted that. No questions asked. I erased the memory of having seen him with my own two eyes and replaced it with the notion that I had only seen someone in a car like his. "You must have an evil twin." I shrugged and let it go.

"Anybody want dessert?" Rose said. "I've got coconut cake."

Then I did the unthinkable. I was so mad at Rose, my own mother, who allowed herself to be unloved and did it so cheerfully that I shoved my chair back rudely and left the table without being excused.

That was when I first began to suspect that it was possible to be so Baptist that you rendered yourself totally unlovable. If she weren't a preacher's secretary, if she weren't always rushing off to church for a wedding or a funeral, would that make her a more interesting woman? Was Daddy defeated before he got started because he believed Rose loved Jesus more than she loved him? Did he wish she'd just become the bride of Christ and left him out of her life completely? I blamed Rose for not being lovable more than I blamed Daddy for not loving her. I always perceived Daddy as the victim in our home—although I never exactly understood how Rose and I got to be the villains. I thought we must have done it by loving Daddy too much. I hoped someday he would forgive us.

If I had written to Jesus it wouldn't have been the sort of love letter Anna wrote. My letter would have said, "Jesus, what in the world is going on here? Why hast thou forsaken me?" There would be so much venom in my heart I would die from it. But I didn't talk about any of that. I locked Anna in the storage room behind my heart and pretended to have lost the key.

## JUST BECAUSE THEY'VE GOT PAPERS DOESN'T MEAN THEY AREN'T STILL DOGS

~~~~~~~~~~~~~~~~~~~~~~~~~~~~~~~~~~~~~~~~~~~~~~~~~~~~

BEFORE WE GO any further let me admit right up front that I don't like Martha anymore, even if her husband is my husband's boss and I know I need to like her for social and political survival. I know it's part of my responsibility—getting along with people who can't be gotten along with. There was a time in my life when I specialized in that. You can ask Brother. He's my husband. He should know.

For a while there I actually thought Martha was my best friend. Anybody would have thought so the way she seemed to look out for me, the way she inserted herself into any matter that even remotely concerned me. But it turns out it was all fake—

maybe it's a California thing, this fakery. Maybe Hollywood has rubbed off on the people out there. I don't know.

It wasn't until Martha's husband, Jeff, began to fire people who'd been in the athletic department since the origin of man that I began to see Martha in a different light. See, everybody knows that Jeff Carter has never made a move in his married life that wasn't sanctioned, approved, and usually initiated by his wife, California Martha. Jeff was named athletic director three years ago and he and Martha moved to town from Hotspot, California, if you know what I mean. Next thing you know lifetime employees of the Western University athletic department were dropping like flies.

Brother, my husband, is not a lifetime employee. He's the football coach. Nothing lifetime about that. It's a no-guarantee, tragic sort of career choice.

Jeff Carter is an ex-athlete himself, which is how he landed the job as athletic director in the first place. But don't believe that notion that *once an athlete always an athlete* like Brother does—he believes all those sports clichés, bless his heart. But I've seen former athletes evolve into the fiercest sorts of businessmen, where admiration of delivering a great hit takes on a whole new meaning, where the final score becomes the profit line and there are grown men in this world who are willing to die for the profit line. Maybe you know some of them?

Jeff played bench-riding pro basketball for a few years in Boston and has been gliding through life on nothing but fumes since then. He was never really a standout. What he was was tall. Extremely tall. Sometimes, I guess, that's enough. People remember his name and he's so tall people are forced to look up to him.

Myself, I don't have a thing against Jeff. As far as I'm concerned he's just a man who over-married. That's all. You know, like a good-natured puppet, whose wife has got all his strings wrapped around her little finger and tied into a tangle of convoluted knots. If you ask me, he's secretly terrified of her. Brother laughed when I said that. Brother has a sense of humor that just won't quit. He can get a good laugh out of just about anything. Unlike me. My sense of humor has sort of deconstructed over the last few years. Now I'm never really sure anymore what's funny and what isn't.

Actually, Martha could pass for a basketball player herself. She is tall too—over six feet. This must have helped them believe they were a perfect couple in the beginning. Maybe it still does. But unlike Jeff, Martha is also overweight. In fact, I'm beginning to see signs of a trend with her. The meaner she is, the fatter she gets. She has to fight it like crazy—the weight. I guess that's justice of a sort. I take what comfort I can in it.

Last week, for example, I ran in to Martha at the bookstore. She was eating an ice-cream cone even though Lord knows how cold it was that day, cold enough to kill probably. Anyway, when I said, "Hey there, Martha," she jumped and put that ice-cream cone behind her back and held it there until I left—like maybe I wouldn't notice that she had something behind her back. If I were meaner I might have said, "What do you have there behind your back, Martha? Show me. Let me see." But I didn't do that because I already knew for one thing and I didn't want to embarrass her or hurt her feelings by making a big thing out of it. I know it's hard to keep the weight off. I've struggled with it a time or two myself. It was odd though. I kept looking for the ice cream to start dripping and making a puddle behind her, but no, I guess even indoors it was too damn cold for anything to melt.

So I just said, "It's good to see you," and went on about my business, which was buying a book I'd heard about called, *How to Be Your Own Best Friend*. I'd already read *When Bad Things Happen to Good People* and *The Road Less Traveled*. Brother looks at the titles of the books I'm reading and just shakes his head. He's not all that much into psychology. He says he thinks I'd be better off reading good murder mysteries.

SO, WHEN MARTHA called me to tell me that one of her rich and interesting friends from California, Wanda Shapiro, had been in a terrible car wreck in Blue River and that the woman's Hollywood movie-tycoon-type husband, Harold Shapiro, had been killed, well, I was stunned. Death always shocks me even if I don't know the people involved. I picture myself in their circumstances. I can practically feel the emotions that go with dying or with watching someone you love die. It's like I've rehearsed this or something.

"Wanda was driving their rented car and Harold was sound asleep in the passenger seat when she hit a serious patch of black ice on the highway," Martha explained. "Of course, when you come from California, there's a good chance you wouldn't know black ice if you saw it. Wanda didn't. Then the car began to slide out of control, you know, the sideways thing when the back wheels try to get ahead of the front wheels. Wanda slammed on the brakes, which is natural enough if you are not used to ice driving, and when she did the car began to spin in tight furious circles and crashed into a state snow-removal vehicle that was parked on the side of the road. Harold was killed instantly."

"That's terrible," I said, momentarily substituting Brother and me for Harold and Wanda. What if people refused to believe it was an accident? What if they thought I drove him to his death on purpose? How would I prove my innocence?

"Wanda isn't even sure Harold ever woke up. She hopes not," Martha said. "Even her screaming, even the crash, none of it woke him up. *Thank God. Thank God. Thank God.* This is all Wanda can say," Martha said. "And Wanda has never been a religious person. It's really tragic."

It seemed Wanda had suffered only minor physical injuries, but was naturally a complete emotional wreck—no pun intended. So she'd called Martha, the only person she knew in the entire Northwest, seeking a little solace and consolation. Martha invited her to come to Crystal Flats and stay with Jeff and her a few days. Stay as long as she liked.

So this was where I came in. Martha wanted me to come over and keep Wanda company while she went out to run some errands. It's football season. This weekend Martha and Jeff are supposed to entertain the members of the Board of Trustees and their wives along with the big-money contributors who keep the Western Gray Wolves in the extras and the artificial goodwill that football teams require. Everything has to be right. I give these sorts of parties myself. I know how it can be to invite people into your home so that they can criticize you and your husband in a friendly, personal way. Of course, the athletic director always has the insulation of the football coach to pad himself with. But the football coach has no insulation at all. That's the main difference.

"I don't think a woman in Wanda's condition should be left alone, Cada," Martha said. "After a thing like this. She's very fragile. She's in a deep depression."

"Okay," I said. "I'll come over. Of course I will." I was doing this for Wanda, woman unmet, unknown—not for Martha, who I was sure, even as we spoke, was plotting some evil for Brother and me. I could feel it anytime I had to breathe the same air she was breathing. And to think I fell for her Christian Women's club routine in the beginning. That's the Southerner in me, I guess. I've been programmed to give religious people the benefit of the doubt. Even though I cannot name for you a single time when it hasn't backfired. Maybe what I should be doing is doubting the benefit. I've gotten sour in recent years. I really hate that about myself. See, winning football games might bring out the best in everybody, but losing games definitely brings out the worst. I've seen the game from both sides these last eight years. It's taken its toll on me too. Everybody says so. So I don't have to look in the mirror to know.

"And, Cada," Martha said, "promise me Brother will win on Saturday. We have to beat Northwest State. Jeff and I are doing the best we can to keep the lid on things, you know. But I don't have to tell you it's not easy these days. I'm sure you read the papers. I'm sure you hear the talk. Nothing helps Brother's cause like a win. So promise me now."

What was I supposed to do? Promise her that Brother would single-handedly win the ball game? Promise her that injured players would miraculously heal and take the field and that Brother would turn too few players into too many, too small players into too big, too slow players into too fast. I said nothing, because here is what I know in my heart. Martha hopes we do lose.

You might not believe me, but I am not a paranoid person. A paranoid coach's wife would be like an underwater bird—unable to survive. I know how to let criticism slide off my ruffled feathers. I know how to get back up when I'm knocked to the ground. What kills me though is knowing Martha likes watching us suffer this way. She likes rubbing salt in the wounds whenever she can. And especially she loves repeating to me any unkind things people say about Brother and me and the win-loss record of the Gray Wolves. I know that Martha is well on her way to getting Brother fired. I know nothing would please her more.

I'd been right by her side, believing she was my true friend, while she maneuvered to get the women's softball coach fired (because she was a lesbian) and two assistant basketball coaches fired (because they were rumored to be having affairs), not to mention all three assistant athletic directors who were here when Jeff was hired, who were guilty of "lacking vision." I know how she works. The way she kills with kindness at first—then whammo, the knife is in your back.

Every time Jeff fires anybody Martha is the first one to go running over to their houses to hug their wives and whisper spiritual messages. She is famous for handing out Bible verses she has scribbled on note cards. "This says it better than I can," she said to Peggy Whitmore when Peggy's husband, Ware, was fired from his job as assistant athletic director, which he'd held for almost twenty-two years. Peggy took the Bible verse in her hand like it was money and she was a beggar. I witnessed the whole thing. And it broke my heart. Martha is the last person in the world Jesus needs to have running around down here performing deeds in his name. Believe me.

Now I get letters from Peggy and Ware, who live somewhere in Arkansas, where Ware got a job at a junior college. Peggy writes, "The people here are nice, but this is just not home, Cada." She knows I understand. I describe the weather here in my letters so maybe she will feel better about Arkansas.

I've tried to warn Brother about Martha, but he won't listen. He thinks I've been reading too much pop psychology. He believes Jeff when Jeff promises to stand by him through this season. He likes Jeff. He has faith in him. He thinks Jeff actually understands the issues of recruiting and injury that plague the Gray Wolves. Brother thinks Jeff is the same sort of strong-minded idealist that he is, but it's not so. Jeff is whatever Martha tells him to be. For all I know she is the one who told him to be tall.

WHEN I ARRIVE at Martha's house she introduces me to Wanda, who has red, red hair and is crying softly into a paper towel. I hug Wanda and she seems shocked and so do I. We don't know each other. In the South people hug all the time, but out West people are not that much into touching each other—especially total strangers. I learned that the hard way. I once grabbed the arm of a professor here during an affectionate moment when our conversation hit a crescendo of confidentiality and confession, just put my hand on his arm, and he nearly jumped out of his skin. He looked at me as though I had just handed him the key to my motel room when what I was trying to say was, "Gee, we're both human beings, isn't this something!" He avoids me like crazy now. So I think for a minute that I should apologize to Wanda—newly widowed and suddenly world-weary. "I can imagine how awful this must be," I said.

"No, you can't," Wanda said. "It's impossible to imagine. I keep thinking I'll wake up in a minute."

"That's how I felt when Lanny died," I said.

"Lanny?"

"I'm sorry," I said. "It's a terrible comparison. Forget I said anything."

"Who's Lanny?" Wanda asked.

"It's a totally different thing," I said.

"Tell me," she insisted. "Who's Lanny?"

"He was our dog." I lowered my head when I spoke. "I'm sorry. It was a terrible thing to say. It's just that we loved him like a person."

"I know," she said. "We have dogs. Two Chinese pugs. His and Hers. That's their names, you know—His and Hers. I keep wondering how I'm ever going to tell them. How do I explain to them that Harold will never be coming home again, will never take them on another walk or whistle for them to come quick and jump up and down for a dog biscuit. They love that."

"They'll read your sadness," I said. "They'll understand. Dogs are so much smarter than we give them credit for."

"Oh my God," Wanda said.

"I know."

"What did you do, you know"—she blew her nose—"when your dog died?"

"I cried. I cried so much I made myself sick and started throwing up. Then I did what you'll do. Keep going. Keep waking up in the morning whether you want to or not. Keep going to bed at night. Keep breathing."

"I don't know if I can."

"You can."

"But I was driving the car," Wanda whispered. "I just keep thinking about that. Harold always insisted on driving, except just this once. He said he was too tired. Wake me up in an hour, he said." Wanda began to choke on her words, like they were objects caught in her throat. "I keep thinking he should have been the one driving—like always—then I'd be dead. Not him. He wasn't supposed to die."

"You two come sit in the kitchen," Martha said, tugging at our arms. "There's coffee."

We sat at the counter in her kitchen and she poured us hot coffee in mugs and we held them to our faces as if they were smoking candles and we were performing some spiritual ritual.

"We're trying to figure out what to do," Martha explained to me. "About Harold's body. They called from Blue River. Want to know what we want done with the body."

"He has to be cremated," Wanda said. "That's what he wanted."

"They can arrange to do that in Blue River," Martha said, "then send Wanda the ashes through the mail."

"But I don't trust the mail," Wanda said. "Not with a thing like this. What if they lose his ashes? What if the box gets crushed and the ashes spill out all over those white letters and bills? His ashes mixed up with advertisements addressed to Occupant? I can't stand to think about it."

"It won't be like that," Martha insisted. "They can mail them special delivery or something."

"I don't want him shipped through the mail like an invitation to a cocktail party." Wanda slammed her coffee cup on the counter, spilling it. "He deserves better."

"They can send his actual body here," Martha said to me. "But we called around this morning and there is no place in Crystal Flats that does cremation. Boulder is the nearest place."

"I think that's what I should do," Wanda said. "Have him shipped to Boulder and cremated there. It's so much closer than Blue River." She stared into her coffee as if she were trying to read an answer at the bottom of the cup. Tears streamed down her face and her nose was running, but she hardly seemed to notice.

"If you want to do that, Wanda," I said, "I'd be happy to drive over to Boulder and pick up his ashes for you. That way you wouldn't have to trust them to the mail. I could deliver them back here to you myself. Safe and sound."

I don't know why I volunteered. I spoke it before I even thought about it. But looking at Wanda, the broken quality of her face, the startled look as if she had just seen a real ghost and her eyes had been glazed over at that precise moment, moved me. Her neediness called out to mine, I guess—and I wanted to help her. I wanted to make something slightly easier for her— almost anything.

"If you mean it, Cada," Martha said, "that would be great. Wouldn't it, Wanda?"

"It would," she said. "Thank you."

"Of course." I smiled. "I'm happy to do it. Really."

"The weather is awful," Wanda reminded me.

"I have four-wheel drive," I said. "I won't hurry. I love the ride to Boulder. I'll just enjoy the scenery and use the time alone to think about things, you know."

"You're sure?" Martha asked.

"I'm sure."

"Let me go call Blue River and tell them to go ahead and ship Harold to Boulder then. They're waiting for us to decide something."

When Martha left the room, Wanda touched my hand. "You know," she said, "I'd really like to ride to Boulder with you. It seems like the right thing to do. I think I should be the one to receive the ashes. It's the least I can do."

"Fine," I said. "That's fine."


WHILE MARTHA RAN her errands Wanda and I sat at the kitchen counter and drank the entire pot of coffee.

"Do you have kids?" she asked me. Usually I really hate that question.

"No," I said.

"We don't either. But now I wish we did. Just sitting here I keep thinking we should have had kids and now it's too late. Everything is too late."

"You have the dogs," I said.

"Right. That's something, I guess."

"And you have friends."

"Yes."

"And how about Harold's parents?"

"Dead."

"Did he love them?"

"I think so. They've been dead a long time."

"Well, you could think about his being reunited with them —with people who loved him. I mean, if that gives you comfort."

"Are you a Baptist or something?" Wanda asked.

"Not exactly," I said.

"I'm Jewish. I don't believe in the afterlife and all that."

"Oh, I'm sorry. I didn't know."

"It's okay," Wanda said.

"What do you believe happens when people die—I mean, if you don't mind me asking."

"Their memory lives on. The dead exist through their influence on the living."

"Oh."

"That's why this life is so important for Jews, you know. No offense. I'm not saying life is not important to Christians."

"Of course not."

"It's just that we don't have the luxury of sitting around waiting on the next life and the promise that everything will be better then. We have to make this life count. Harold did. He made his life count. He didn't have anything but dreams when I met him. And he died a wealthy and respected man. He had wonderful friends too. People loved him, they really did."

"You must have really loved him too," I said.

"I was his wife."

"Right."

"He build Shapiro Productions practically single-handedly into a major film-production company. He left me without financial worries. But God, already, I'm so lonely. And worse, I'm guilty. I would be happier if I was the dead one and he had been driving the car." She began to cry softly.

"That wouldn't be better," I said. "It would be better if neither of you were dead."

"I'll have Harold's ashes, of course." She rubbed at the tears under her eyes with a trembling finger. "I'll save a bit of them —always—in a drawer of something, just for me. And the rest, I've been thinking. I'll put some out on his favorite golf course—he loved golf. And I'll put some in the ocean because he loved the ocean. And I'll sprinkle some in the yard around the house—just to, I don't know, just to know he's somehow near. Is that crazy?"

"It's lovely."

Wanda rubbed her crumpled paper towel over her face. Her mascara smeared across her eyes like two huge black Xs.

"It's funny," I said. "I've always said if Brother died I'd sprinkle his ashes on the golf course and the football field."

"Really?"

"Yes. Except, of course, he doesn't want to be cremated. He wants to be buried. Back in Georgia. In that good red clay."

"You mean you've already thought about your husband dying?"

"I guess so. I mean I haven't planned his death, you know. It's just sort of crossed my mind."

"Why?"

"Why? I don't know. I thought it must cross everybody's mind sometime or another."

"I mean it's none of my business. But it's just that I never thought about Harold dying. Never. He was always healthy and all. He was always so full of life. I just never thought about anything like this happening."

"It's just as well," I said. "You can't really prepare for a death, can you? All you can do is accept it."

"I guess so."

"That's all you can do."

"What if your husband died suddenly?" Wanda asked. "What would you do?"

"I don't know," I said. "Don't get me wrong. I don't sit around thinking about Brother dying and figuring out what I would do if he did—planning my life as a widow or anything like that. Actually, I hardly ever think about him dying. Mostly I just think about divorcing him. He stays alive the whole time. It's just a divorce. I imagine that I've left him and it's during the season and he never even noticed that I was gone. Sometimes I wonder how long it would take him to miss me. I wonder if he would miss me at all. That's all I mean. It's perfectly normal to wonder."

"Why do you think he wouldn't miss you?"

"He's married to his job mostly. Football, you know. I hardly ever see him—I mean, really see him. His job is, well, everything, you know."

"I've never been to a football game."

"Never?"

"No."

"Never once in your whole life? Not even when you were a kid?"

"Never."

"Oh my gosh," I said. "I've never met a person who has never been to a single football game in her whole life. It's amazing. If you ask me you're a lucky woman."

"Harold didn't like football."

"You're kidding?"

"No. He didn't like any sports except golf. And he only liked to play it. He hated to watch it. Harold wasn't much of a spectator, you know. He was a doer."

"Well, don't get me wrong about Brother. He's a great guy."

"I'm sure he is."

"Maybe you'll meet him sometime."

"Maybe so," Wanda said. "I'm going to the game with Martha on Saturday if I'm up to it. She invited me."

"You should go," I said. "It might take your mind off things for a couple of hours."

"I doubt it," she said.

WHEN I ARRIVED to pick up Wanda for the drive to Boulder to get Harold's ashes she opened the front door and said, "Martha has decided to come with us. That's okay, isn't it?"

"Of course," I said, although it was not okay. It was the last thing I wanted—all day in the car with Martha, fake friend and masterful manipulator of misery. "I'll wait out in the car," I said. "I've got the heater going."

Don't get me wrong. I didn't like disliking Martha. It came unnaturally to me and I resisted it, but it was like resisting the cold weather. Either you prepare for the damage you know it can do you and proceed cautiously, or else, like a fool, you freeze to death and everybody blames you entirely for your lack of good judgment. It was awful, really. I hated it. Not the cold weather, but the coldheartedness that was overtaking me lately. I thought of Martha as a Chinook wind that could blow Brother and me right out of this life as we know it. I'd heard stories of Chinook winds that blew stopped trains off their tracks. That's sort of what the Gray Wolves were like this year. A train stopped in its tracks. Anybody with half a brain knew it was not stopped forever. I just thought of this as a refueling stop. That's all. But I knew Martha had other plans. She was plotting for the train to jump the tracks—then she'd help Jeff find a new engineer and pretend to be heartbroken when Brother and I were left out in the cold. She'd smile and wave to us from the caboose. I was psychic about this.

When I saw Wanda and Martha making their way down the shoveled walk to the car my heart sank. Martha was bringing her Bible with her. I had the urge to throw the Bronco into first and accelerate down the icy road before they could get into the car. I don't know what stopped me.

Martha got in the front passenger seat and Wanda got in the back seat. I hadn't gotten as far as the end of the block when Martha said, "Cada, let's stop a minute and say a prayer."

"Now?"

"Yes. Pull over," Martha said.

I slowed the car to a crawl. When I had the car stopped Martha took my hand and reached over the seat for Wanda's hand. "Let's pray," she said. "Dear Jesus . . ."

"Actually," I said, "Wanda is Jewish, you know. She might not want to do this."

"I don't mind," Wanda said. "If it makes you two feel better."

"I'll change the words," Martha said. "Dear God, please be with us today as we travel in this bad weather. Please watch over and guide us. Be with Wanda today during this ordeal. And help us know how to comfort her. Amen."

"That was nice," Wanda said.

I shifted the car into first and inched out into the cold world.

"Go slow," Martha said. "This is not easy for Wanda, traveling on these icy roads. It reminds her, you know."

"I'll be careful," I said. "Wanda, you tell me if you want me to slow down or stop or anything."

"How far is it to Boulder?" Wanda asked.

"Three hours on good roads, at least four on icy ones," I said. "But the scenery is beautiful. Nothing but mountains and antelope. It's restful in a deserted sort of way."

"Deserted," Wanda said. "That's how I feel."

WE STOPPED AT Hardee's for hot coffee in large paper cups. I don't drive anywhere without coffee. Then we slid out of town and got on the highway that would lead us out into the nothingness that the West is so famous for. Miles of it. Miles and miles of not-people. I'd come to love that.

"I had the most terrible thought last night," Wanda said as the town slipped out of sight behind us. "Tell me if you think this is terrible. I thought that maybe when I got Harold's ashes I'd take a spoonful of them and stir them into a cup of soup or something and you know, eat them, swallow his ashes as a way of keeping him with me. Is that terrible?"

"It sounds like an advertisement for Metamucil," I said. "No offense."

"I bet ashes are a natural laxative," Martha said. "They might not actually stay with you."

"It's symbolic," Wanda said. "That's all. It's a gesture. Don't you see?"

"If you think it will make you feel better," I said, "then I say do it."

"You don't think it sounds cannibalistic?" Wanda asked.

"It sounds like a little-known love ritual," I said. "You're probably not the first person to ever think of it. I bet you'd be surprised what people think of in times of grief."

"So you don't think it's sick then?"

"You're heartsick," I said. "Maybe swallowing a spoonful of Harold's ashes will make you feel better. Like medicine. Think of it that way."

"I haven't decided yet whether or not to do it," Wanda said. "It just crossed my mind. I've been having lots of crazy thoughts."

"What else?" Martha asked.

"Well." Wanda choked on a swallow of her coffee and put her napkin over her mouth while she coughed. "I have these secrets," she said finally, tears welling in her eyes.

"What do you mean, secrets?" I asked, staring at her swollen face in the rearview mirror.

"Secrets that I never told Harold. Secrets that I kept from him."

"Everybody has secrets," Martha said. She was sitting sideways in the front seat and twisted herself around to pat Wanda's trembling hand.

"Not everybody has secrets like this." Wanda shook her head, crying softly into her wadded napkin. "Now that Harold's dead I regret not telling him everything, you know. I swore to myself someday I would tell him, but then, the time never seemed right. I was afraid the truth would ruin everything."

"You did it out of love," Martha said, quietly. "Harold would understand that."

"I did it out of fear. I was afraid if he knew everything he would stop loving me. He would leave me." Wanda began to cry in sobs and buried her face in her hands. We rode along in silence and let her cry. We rode for what seemed like a hundred miles.

"It can't be that awful," I said finally. "You never killed anybody, did you?" I tried to put a light touch on things—which used to be one of my best qualities.

She began to cry harder, gasping for air.

"You killed somebody?" I said. Suddenly it occurred to me that it was possible. After all, she was from L.A., where, according to Martha, the people are fast and wild.

"I had an affair." Wanda lifted her head and looked at Martha and me like we might slam on the brakes, screech to a halt, and insist she get out of the car and walk the rest of the way to Boulder in the snow now that we knew what a wretched woman she really was. I kept my eyes on the road straight ahead, both hands on the wheel.

"God forgives," Martha said. "Listen to me, Wanda. An affair is not an unpardonable sin."

I wondered how Martha knew this with such certainty.

"You don't understand," Wanda wept. "It wasn't just an overnight thing. I had an affair for three years."

"I'm sure you had your reasons," I said.

"Well," Martha said, "three years *is* a long time."

"Harold and I were only married for fifteen years," Wanda said. "Subtract those three and it's only twelve years. It's like I stole three years of his life from him. I hate myself for that."

"Maybe he had affairs too," I said, hopeful. "Maybe he kept secrets from you too. I bet he did."

"I wish I could believe that." Wanda blew her nose.

"Forgive yourself," Martha said. "That's all you can do."

"Who was the guy?" I asked her. "I mean, you must have cared for him if you kept it up for three years."

"I can't tell you his name. You've heard of him."

"You mean he's a movie star?" I said.

"Sort of," Wanda said. "He's an actor."

"Oh my gosh." My imagination conjured up an assortment of chiseled faces on the silver screen.

"It would have killed Harold if he'd known," Wanda said.

"Well, he didn't know and it didn't kill him," Martha said. "That's the important thing. God forgives. Remember that."

"Did you love this guy—this famous actor?" I asked.

"I did," Wanda said. "At first. I thought I would leave Harold and marry this man. He was exciting, you know. And he said he loved me. He talked all the good talk—that's what really got me. It was like I completely forgot what an actor he was and I just went headfirst into believing him. Now I don't know if I really loved him or if I just loved the idea that he loved me."

"What about the sex?" I asked.

"Cada!" Martha said. "For heaven's sake! You're talking to a fresh widow here."

"It's okay," Wanda said. "I need to confess everything. The sex wasn't that great. He was too fast, you know. He did all this talking in bed, long drawn-out fantasies he liked to talk about. You know, even in bed it was like he was auditioning for a part. It turned him on. But me, I swear, sometimes it was like hearing a bedtime story when you're a little girl, and the story, designed to amuse you, really puts you into a deep sleep instead. It's awful to say. I mean, I'm revising things now, looking back."

"And Harold never suspected a thing?"

"That's not the worst part." Wanda put her hand up against the glass of the window, as if she were staring at her wedding ring—which happened to be a huge diamond—on the hand of a perfect stranger. She spread her fingers and looked at her hand a long time. "I got pregnant," Wanda whispered. "It wasn't Harold's baby. It was the other man's."

"You don't have to tell us this," Martha said, turning in her seat to face forward, straight ahead at the long straight road in front of us, to avoid looking at Wanda's contorted, confessional face —the one I was staring at in the rearview mirror, the one I couldn't take my eyes off of.

"What did you do?" I asked.

"I decided to have the baby, you know. I wanted a baby. When I told the man, he just kept saying over and over, *Jayne is going to kill me, Jayne is going to kill me. What am I going to tell Jayne.* It was so awful—the way he reacted, like his penis was the arrow on a compass and he suddenly remembered it was always supposed to be pointing north, and Jayne was North.

"Isn't that just like a man," I said, as if I were an expert on such things. It was something I thought I might have liked to be an expert on.

"I was so hurt," Wanda continued. "I didn't know what to do. So I decided to tell Harold the baby was his. Just lie. I was so lonely then, I guess, and confused. I thought a baby might fix things between Harold and me. I thought it could bring us closer."

"Who was Jayne?" I asked.

"The man's wife," Wanda said. "Until the moment I got pregnant he'd claimed he hated her. He said his marriage was a big mistake and he was just waiting for the right minute to get out of it once and for all. He swore for three years that he'd never loved his wife, that she sort of tricked him into marrying her by acting so needy. And I believed him. I felt sorry for him. Can you believe that?"

"You can't blame yourself," Martha said. "It's not your fault he was a coward."

"When I saw how he panicked, when I saw the way he ran back to his wife and hid up underneath her skirt, I don't know, it just killed me." Wanda's voice broke as she spoke. "All that time I thought he loved me. Now it all sounds so ridiculous."

"So what did you do?" I asked again.

"I quit thinking of him the same way after that. I couldn't get my feelings back for him. It was like he shrank so small that he sort of became invisible to me. So I called him and told him there had been a mistake—that the baby was Harold's. He said, 'Thanks. Wanda, I appreciate this. Really. I won't forget it. I swear.'"

"What a guy," I said.

"I haven't seen him since. He called me a couple of times after that to see if I would meet him, for old times' sake, he said. Here I was pregnant and he was calling me with all this *baby, baby, sweet baby* talk. He said he missed me. He said he still loved me. Each time I hung up the phone after he called me I would throw up. I mean I would vomit until I was so empty that I was afraid I might harm the baby inside me."

"So what about his wife? This Jayne?"

"He's still married to her."

"That must hurt," I said.

"It doesn't," Wanda said. "Now I think they're perfect for each other. They sort of deserve each other, you know."

"So then what happened?"

"I told Harold about the baby. I was crying the whole time, which he thought was because I was scared. God, he was so happy. You should have seen him. It changed things between us, you know. He started coming home early, watching what I ate, buying me maternity clothes. He was so sweet to me. So excited. So I began to feel better. I started planning the nursery. I'd almost started thinking everything had worked out for the best after all. I was close to happy then, I really was. Then, in my fourth month, something went wrong. I started bleeding, you know, suddenly. It felt so wrong. I knew I was being punished— I knew I deserved to be punished. I miscarried. Lost the baby. Nearly lost my mind."

"But you didn't lose Harold," Martha said.

"No," Wanda said. "Not until now."

"You're not being punished by Harold's death," Martha said. "Even if it seems like it, you're not. God doesn't work like that."

"Harold and I tried to get pregnant again, but we never could. And I never told him the truth."

"It doesn't matter now," I said. "Your secret is safe."

"You must think I'm awful," Wanda said. "I had to tell someone. If I didn't tell someone I think it would kill me."

"I know what you mean," Martha said almost dreamily. "I had an affair once."

We came over the crest of a hill at that moment, and before us lay what looked like shining grease on the road. We hit the stretch of black ice at decent dry-road speed and without thinking I instinctively tapped the brake. "Oh, shit," I said. I felt the rear wheels beginning to swerve back and forth, like the car was a full-bodied woman with a swaggering sway of the hips. I tried to turn the steering wheel in the direction of the slide, the backfield in motion, but the sliding was too fast. "Hold on!" I yelled.

"Oh my God!" Wanda screamed. I looked in the rearview mirror just in time to see her close her eyes and slip low in the seat. When the car began to spin I heard her roll to the floor. She made a thud, like a dead body after a bullet to the heart.

We spun in furious, wobbly circles down the middle of the iced highway. It was like being at the fair and finding yourself on a ride that is advertised as wild and exciting but is really designed to kill. Something about the spinning was comforting to me. Like we were in the spin cycle of a spiritual washing machine and all our sins were being spun out of us momentarily. I felt the splash of cold coffee cover me and heard Martha shriek as we spiraled around and around, faster and faster, until we slid off the edge of the road and came to a sudden abrupt halt in the deep snow on the shoulder of the highway. The spinning had splattered coffee all over us and when the car stopped and we looked at each other it was like a murder had happened and we were all guilty and covered with the blood of the innocent.

"We're okay," I insisted, laying my head against the steering wheel. "I'm sorry. I didn't see the ice in time. I'm sorry."

"Nobody's hurt," Martha said. Mid-sip, her cup of coffee had splashed over her face, and now she patted at the dripping mess with her hands.

We turned to check on Wanda. She was lying on the floorboard of the back seat. "It's okay," I said, leaning over the seat reaching for her, stroking her hair as she cried. "I'm so sorry," I said again and again. "We hit ice. We're okay, Wanda. Really, we're okay."

Martha took Wanda's hand and helped her up onto the seat. "See," Martha said, "it just shows you that black ice can sneak up on anybody. Accidents don't always happen because of carelessness, sometimes they just happen because of conditions. Maybe this was God's way of making sure you know this, you know, that the accident that killed Harold wasn't your fault. Cada is a good driver—really—but she can't control bad weather and ice on the road any more than you could. See?"

I felt tears come to my eyes when Martha said this. I don't ordinarily think of myself as one of God's teaching devices. Listening to Martha, I thought I might succumb to some secret grief of my own if I wasn't careful. "I'm going to get out and look at the car," I said, "see if there's any damage."

While Martha comforted Wanda and helped her sit up and got out Kleenex to wipe away the coffee splatters covering both of them, I walked to the hood of the car and squatted down as if to check the tires, but instead I put my head against the bumper of the car and let out several huge gulping cries that hurt my chest, like my heart was a frozen iceberg, the tip of which stabbed me with each sob I took. Was I having a heart attack? I caught my breath long enough to see that there was a dent in the fender of the car where we had hit a mile marker, but no other visible damage. If I was lucky I could put the Bronco in reverse and back my way out of this snowbank. I wiped my face with my gloves, took a deep breath, and got back in the car.

"YOU LOOK LIKE you've been shot," Martha said, handing me a fistful of Kleenex. My sweater was stained with coffee. It was easy to imagine it was blood. I swiped at the spots absent-mindedly.

Wanda was sitting in the back with her legs stretched out longways on the seat, gripping the box of Kleenex in her lap. "Are you okay?" I asked her. She nodded. "I promise I'll get you to Boulder safely," I said. "I'll go slower too."

"We're a mess," Martha said, looking at her own wet hair and coffee-damaged makeup in the mirror. "We look like we've just come home from war."

I started the car and put it in reverse and with no trouble at all eased the Bronco backward on the divergent path it had made into the deep snow. In no time we were back on the deserted highway, making our cautious way through the ice patches on the blacktop.

"If we're on our way home from war," Wanda said, "let's pretend we won the stupid war. Let's pretend we're all heroes."

"That's the spirit," Martha said.

We had driven less than a mile when Wanda tapped Martha's shoulder and said, "Did you say you had an affair too?"

Martha ran her fingers through her hair like they were the prongs on a rake. "No." She smiled. "I was going to say that *if* I ever had an affair, I would forgive myself. And you should too. That's all."

"Oh," Wanda said. "I could have sworn . . ."

WHEN WE FINALLY pulled up in the parking lot of the mortuary a silence fell over us. I parked very carefully and as close to the door as I could get. Wanda was staring out the window like she expected to see Harold—or his ghost, at least—walk out to meet us.

"If you want to wait here," I said, "I'll go in and get his ashes and bring them out to you. It might be easier on you that way."

"No," Wanda said. "I have to go inside. I'll probably have to sign papers or something."

"They'll want your credit card number," Martha said. "They said so on the phone."

"Come with me," Wanda said, "both of you."

We tried to patch our wilted and stained selves together. We glanced in our compacts and patted our faces with powder and put on fresh lipstick and in the end looked no better at all— maybe worse. "Let's go," Martha said. "Nobody cares how we look."

The minute the mortuary door closed behind us Wanda made a whimpering noise that caused Martha and me to grab her arms to keep her from collapsing onto the floor. "I don't know if I can do this," Wanda whispered.

The man who came out of the office to greet us seemed well practiced in dealing with the grief-stricken. "We're here for Harold Shapiro's ashes," I said.

"This way, ladies," he said, motioning us to follow him. He led us to a small sitting room where classical music was being softly pumped into the air like an auditory anesthetic. "Have a seat." We obeyed him silently, all three of us sitting in a line on the sofa, holding hands, trying not to breathe too deeply and suck in any more of the death vapors than we had to. "Which of you is Mrs. Shapiro?" the man asked.

Wanda raised her hand as if she were a child who knew the right answer to the teacher's question. "She is," I said.

"Very well," he smiled. "Can I get you ladies some coffee?"

We had already been doused in coffee, were still wearing a thin coating of it on our skin and clothes. "No thank you," we said in unison.

The man left the room and came back minutes later with official forms for Wanda to sign. She gave him her American Express card and her California driver's license. "You're a long way from home," he said. "How do you like this weather?"

She closed her eyes as a way of answering him. It was an answer he seemed to understand. He left the room again, the signed papers in hand, and when he returned he was carrying a small brown paper bag—the kind they use in grocery stores. He reached inside the bag and pulled out an equally nondescript brown cardboard box that was sealed with packing tape. On the front of the bag and on the top of the box were computer print-out, peel-off stickers that read SHAPIRO, HAROLD T.

The man handed the box to Wanda. "I'm sorry," he said, as if apologizing for the low-budget quality of the packaging of Harold's ashes. "You're sure you aren't interested in purchasing a more suitable container?" he said. "We have some lovely urns I could show you."

Wanda shook her head no. She had let go of our hands in order to receive Harold's ashes, but Martha and I kept a tight grip on each of her arms. We stood and pulled her gently until she was standing. She was staring at the box inside the bag. She was staring at the words SHAPIRO, HAROLD T.

"Are you ready to go?" I asked.

She nodded.

"Let's get out of here," Martha said.

On our way back to the car we walked across the icy parking lot as slowly as was humanly possible, like somehow it was wrong that we were being allowed to leave carrying the remains of a full-grown man in a container smaller than a shoe box. It felt like we were the worst sort of thieves. Wasn't someone going to come running after us to say there had been some terrible mistake? Shouldn't a man like Harold produce enough ashes to fill, say, a large suitcase, at least? It felt like when I was a kid and used to play hide-and-seek, but sometimes, no matter what the rules of the game were, I didn't really want to hide successfully, what I really wanted was to be found, to be easy to find and therefore be found quickly. But no one came after us today. The imaginary seeker I wished for and hoped for—that probably Wanda and Martha wished for too—was not coming after us.

As we reached our car we passed a family of mourners who had arrived in a long black limousine. A weeping couple got out of the back seat and family members gathered around them as if to prop them up and herd them inside. I knew instantly, just by looking at them, that they had lost a child. They were crying and holding handkerchiefs over their faces so that it seemed impossible that they could see where they were going—or that they even cared anymore.

The sight of them clinging to each other, the man crying as loudly as the woman, the way they had to be pushed forward by their loved ones, was too much for Wanda. She stopped dead still in the parking lot and watched the procession go by. She pressed Harold's ashes hard to her chest and for the first time all day she let herself go, shouting, "This is not fair. It's not fair. I can't stand this." She curved her body around the tiny box that was Harold now, her spine curling like a sea creature around its prey, like a shell around the meat of the nut. She might have fallen to the ground if Martha and I had let her. Gravity was pulling on her so hard, sucking her down, down. But we refused to let go of her, refused to let her fall.

The grieving couple glanced at her with such a startled and knowing look, then turned back to each other, the woman gripping the lapels of the man's coat, the man with both his arms wrapped around the woman.

"Harold!" Wanda shouted. "Harold!" She was looking around desperately, as if she were expecting him to get out of the limousine next, as if he would come running when he heard her call his name. Martha and I tried to smother her pain with our bodies. We opened our coats and wrapped them around her like a tent, like she was lost in the wilderness and we were determined to be her safe refuge. She struggled against us, gripping the boxed Harold, hitting at us with him, but we hung tough, we pressed ourselves against her until her thrashing stopped. It was as if her grief were a fire and it was our job not to let it rage out of control. "Why is this happening?" Wanda shouted. "Not Harold. Please, God, not Harold!"

Martha and I pulled Wanda to the car. We were crying too, Wanda's grief having ignited our own. It seemed to me that I loved Harold as much as she did—under the circumstances, since I had never been unfaithful to him, maybe I loved him even more—it seemed I had known him all my life, that I had meant to tell him everything important too, that I would hardly be able to continue living in a world that he was no longer part of.

We helped Wanda into the back seat and for a moment, I took Harold in the now crushed cardboard box gently from her hands, I held him to my own breast, I bent my head and kissed the box lightly. I held him as though, in death, he was a newborn infant and I was volunteering—no, I was insisting—on being allowed to love him, to be his mother maybe, or his sister, or the love of his life whom he had managed to let get away from him as a young man, which he had regretted every day of his life since. Harold, this man I never met, had needed me, and I had let him down. I needed another chance.

When Wanda was settled in the back seat of the car I handed

Harold back to her and she sat staring straight ahead with him in her lap like he was a sack lunch and she was on her way to the saddest picnic of her life.

WHEN LANNY DIED it was February. Brother was out of town and couldn't get home because of a blizzard that closed the airports. He cried when I told him I'd found Lanny dead that morning—he'd died while he slept at the foot of our bed. His body was already getting cold when I woke up and touched him. I'd sat and brushed his fur until there wasn't a tangle in it. It shone. Then I called Brother, who was off recruiting. I loved Brother for the way he cried when I told him. He cried just as bad as I was crying.

I wanted to wait for Brother to help me bury Lanny in the side yard underneath the crab-apple tree that at the moment looked like a gray skeleton, the wind whipping through it, banging the branches together like so many bones rattling. I waited for three days with Lanny's body in the freezer in the basement, where I could open it up anytime I wanted to and whisper a message and touch his frozen body just to be sure.

The vet tried to get me to have Lanny cremated, but I refused. I wanted him to stay whole. I don't like the idea, you know, of a formerly living creature put into an oven, like a rump roast you are intentionally going to burn into a lump of charcoal. It doesn't sit right with me. I don't care if death is more manageable that way. Back home we bury our family and pets in the warm earth. We wrap them in a blanket of red dirt and maybe plant an azalea or a dogwood sapling to mark the grave. I like knowing my loved ones are planted like that, in the good earth, where if left untended their grave will sprout a tangle of blackberries or dandelions or wild onions—like their spirit rising up or something. I like that idea a lot.

So I took Brother's wood ax and went outside and began chopping at the hard crust of ice that covered our so-called yard. I just wanted to bust it up, you know, get down below the frozen part to where the real earth was. Ice is hard, though. It really is. I couldn't do it. I chopped at the ground for the longest time. My elderly neighbor said later she saw me out there with that ax for over two hours—she was afraid I would give myself a heart attack she said, which was why she called the police. She has since apologized. More than once. When the officers drove up in their official car I didn't know what to think. They just sat there and stared at me for the longest time, so I kept on chopping. There's nothing illegal about that, is there? Maybe the temperature was dangerously low, but is this a free country or isn't it? Finally they got out and escorted me into my own house. It was either that, they said, or they would have to call the mental health people. It was like they thought I was a crazy woman or something.

I wasn't even tired because I was fueled by the worst sort of heartache. We'd had Lanny almost seventeen years. I couldn't remember life without him. Brother gave Lanny to me the first Christmas we were married. He was supposed to help get us ready for the children we would have later, you know, be like a warm-up for parenthood. But no children ever came. It was like getting your house full of candy for Halloween, decorating everything and being ready. But no trick-or-treaters ever knock at your door. Not one. You keep looking out your window and you see that there are kids in costumes across the street ringing doorbells, little monsters and princesses and space aliens, but they don't come to your house. You don't know why. You call out to them, you invite them, but they still don't come. It breaks your heart, but you finally decide it must just be one of the mysteries of life. You have to decide that. You have no choice. It's either that or start hating yourself—or the world.

But the trouble with one of life's mysteries is that it can be like a dormant little seed deep inside you. Like you can actually be pregnant with one of life's mysteries. I know. It happened to me. I was swollen with it, the mystery, pregnant with a huge empty space that I wanted to be freed of. It was like hoping to give birth to a beautiful answer to your prayers, but instead, no matter how you labor, you only deliver a small and quivering question.

So it's like when Halloween is over, when you know it is way too late for any child to come to your well-lit door—then there is nothing for you to do but eat all that individually wrapped candy yourself. You just fill yourself up with it, like jamming stuffing into a hollow thing. It felt like that. Maybe I thought if I ate myself fat, that then my body would understand what I needed, you know, like a signal—then maybe I could buy one more pregnancy test at Osco and it would be positive. Finally positive. I don't know if Brother ever really understood all this, how swollen I was with emptiness—but Lanny did. He used to lay his head in my lap and together we would listen to the growling emptiness.

Brother had his team to be his kids. He was known to say things like, "I may not have the best win-loss record in the conference, but I got the best kids. There's no better kids in the world." He loved his players. He fathered them better than lots of men father their natural offspring.

Maybe teaching school should have given me that same sort of satisfaction, but it didn't. Maybe something was wrong with me. I don't know. But I wanted to bathe a baby in the kitchen sink, you know. Wake up in the night with milk leaking from my breasts and nurse my crying child. I wanted to take him for his first haircut or buy her her first tea set, which would not be plastic but actual breakable china. I wanted the first tooth, the first step, and the first day of school.

Next thing you know I was bathing Lanny almost once a week and clipping his toenails and tying bows around his neck. No matter what else there wasn't—there was always Lanny. You could count on Lanny if you couldn't count on anything else in this life. He was part poodle too and smarter than most people I knew.

It was summer before the ground was soft enough for us to dig his grave. By then the crab-apple tree was as green as it could be, like a beautiful leaf cloud floating over Lanny's final resting place.

WE DROVE FOR almost an hour in total silence. Wanda had composed herself and seemed almost at peace, glancing out the windows at the senseless world sliding by.

"Maybe we should stop for lunch?" Martha said. "It's almost two o'clock and we haven't eaten anything all day. You need to eat something, Wanda. You need to keep up your strength."

"We can go to a drive-through in Fort Collins," I said. "Get a hamburger. We don't even have to get out of the car."

"No," Wanda said. "Let's stop. Let's have a nice lunch somewhere."

"Really?" I said.

"We could go to Bananas," Martha said. "It's not far. It's pleasant."

"You're sure you're up to it, Wanda?" I asked.

"I'm sure," she said. "And I'm hungry."

We parked at the mall. It seemed a million miles away from the mortuary. It seemed to signal our return to the real world— our successful escape from the insistent world beyond or, in Wanda's case, the insistent not-world beyond.

"Should I take Harold in or leave him in the car?" Wanda asked. It seemed like such a huge decision.

"I can lock the car if you want to leave him," I said.

"It would be so awful, though," Martha said, "if we came out and found somebody had broken into the car and stolen him, thinking he was something else, you know."

"Nobody in his right mind steals ashes," I said.

"A thief might not realize it's ashes until he gets home with it," Martha said. "You know how sick the criminal mind is. When he sees he has a sack of ashes, then what?"

"We could hide them under the seat," I said. "Or we could put them down in the spare-tire compartment with the jack and all—just until we get back from lunch."

"I'll take him with me," Wanda said. "I'll feel better if I can see Harold's ashes with my own two eyes and know they're safe."

When the waiter showed us to our table for four Wanda sat Harold's ashes in the fourth chair. We all piled our coats in the chair first and she sat him on top of the coats so we could see him the whole time. It made me think of putting a child in a booster seat—because it's important to be able to watch a child, and because children get into less mischief when they can see the top of the table than when they can only see underneath it—where it is dark and their imaginations can go wild. Wanda arranged the sack containing Harold just right, front label facing the table. She patted it and we all took our seats.

At lunch Wanda ordered wine. I was glad. I didn't order any because I was driving and it had begun to snow again and the roads were already sheets of ice and we'd nearly come to catastrophe once already when I was stone sober. Martha didn't order any wine because she doesn't believe in drinking. She thinks it's evil. I'd heard her say so, but she didn't say so now, thank goodness. "Wine is a good idea," I said to Wanda. "It will do you good."

When her wine came Wanda lifted her glass and Martha and I lifted our Diet Cokes and Wanda said, "To women who understand." She tapped our glasses. "I'll always remember today, the way the two of you have helped me."

"And to Harold," I said as an afterthought, "who lived a good life." We all glanced at the man in the bag and lifted our glasses in his honor.

"Cada would have liked Harold, wouldn't she, Martha?" Wanda said. "Too bad she never got to meet him."

"It's funny," I said, "but after today I almost feel like I know him—or, you know, *knew* him."

"Do you have a picture in your billfold?" Martha asked. "Show her his picture."

While Wanda fumbled through her purse, we ordered from the menu, soups, salads, and pastas. I secretly wanted to order red meat—a filet maybe or a prime rib—but it seemed wrong. Red meat is man food, and there was only the spirit of a man with us—or in Wanda's case, the memory of a man. She handed me a photograph. "Here," she said, "this is Harold—*was* Harold. It's not really a very good picture. He was much better looking in real life, wasn't he, Martha?"

"He was distinguished looking," Martha said. "Not a pretty boy, but you know, dignified."

The picture was of a gray-haired man significantly older than Wanda who was sitting in what looked like a kitchen chair with two dogs in his lap. "Oh," I said, "this must be His and Hers."

"Aren't they precious?" Wanda said. "I miss them." She sipped her wine. "I know they're not going to understand when I come home alone, without Harold. They love Harold so much."

"I can see that," I said. "Harold looks like a nice guy," I said. I could not make myself grasp the fact that the man hugging his dogs in this picture in my hand was now a small heap of ashes confined to a paper bag sitting on a pile of coats and scarves while his widow and two friends—one of whom he'd never seen in his life—ordered nourishment and sustenance from a bountiful menu.

I handed the photo back to Wanda. She was telling Martha about her financial condition. It sounded to me like something out of a fairy tale. King dies and leaves his queen his castle and the keys to his kingdom and guardianship of his two Chinese pugs, His and Hers. "I don't know if I should sell the house and look for something smaller," she said. "A house that size for just one person is crazy. Besides, I'm afraid to stay alone there. I always have been. That sounds silly, doesn't it?"

If Brother died, I wondered, how long would it take me to pay off our credit cards? I wondered if I would live long enough. Maybe I'd go back to teaching school again. I'd quit a few years ago when I'd run out of optimism on all fronts and when it seemed to me that not only was my love of teaching irrevocably damaged, but teaching was fast becoming an insultingly low-esteemed profession—it had always been insultingly low-paid. The last couple of years I had kids carrying guns to class and committing murders and suicides on the weekends and popping pills the way, when I was a kid, we used to pop caps. I didn't know how to relate. I didn't know how to make them care about themselves or anybody else. I didn't seem to know how to do anything that helped them in any significant way, so I decided to quit and open up space for a teacher who might know better how to do that, who might not be spent, bent, and burnt out, like me. No, I wouldn't go back to teaching. I'd have to find something else.

Brother would want to be buried in Georgia. I don't blame him. That's home. Everybody who loves him is there. They're definitely not out here. The truth is we'd lived through football seasons where Brother had died tragic deaths week after week, first on the football field on Saturdays, then in the press on Sundays. This double-death routine took its toll on him, but come Monday morning he had always risen from the dead and was on his way to the office. "You can't keep a good man down," I'd say as he went out the door. "You mean you can't keep a fool out of foolishness," he'd say, and smile at me. Brother can always smile. People out here really hate that.

Some seasons Brother went about town like a ghost. I'd seen entire restaurants go silent when he entered. I'd seen children recognize him and run to their mother and grab her hand. I'd seen drivers crash into the car in front of them when they saw Brother walking down the street on his way to speak to the Quarterback Club on Mondays at lunchtime—this walking dead man who still had a few things left to say. (Although nothing much really left to say to me.)

I'd lived through whole seasons where I'd been treated like a widow, the hugs from the die-hard fans, the pats on the shoulder, the flowers with notes saying, "So sorry you're having to go through this," the averted eyes and sad faces and relentless sympathy—not to mention the ugly chants, personal slurs, beers spilt down my back, and hate mail.

So maybe suffering all these little deaths of Brother's would make it easier on me to face the big one when it came. Who knows. This was what I know about Brother. Even when he's been killed—on the field or off—he is always still alive. And even when he is most alive, he is always a little bit dead.

"You'll be lonely," Martha said to Wanda, "but at least you won't have to worry about money."

"Maybe I'll travel," Wanda said, "for a while. Just until I get used to the idea that Harold's gone—dead." She shook her head. "I have to learn to say the word. *Dead*. He's *dead*. Harold is *dead*." She looked at the battered paper sack beside her. "You're *dead*, Harold," she said. "I'm so sorry." Then she took a big swallow of her white wine. Wanda had only had one glass so far, but it seemed like more.

"What about the dogs?" I said. "If you travel—"

"I can arrange to take them."

"Where will you go?"

"Northern Spain, maybe. Or the coast of Spain. It's beautiful there."

"I'd go to Hawaii." Martha took a sip of her Diet Coke, then slammed the glass on the table. "No, I take that back. I'm past bathing-suit vacations. I'm too old for that. I'm too fat. I'd go to Paris. I'd go to a different museum every day and a different café every evening. I'd take long walks and listen to music and read all the books I've never read."

"What would you do, Cada?" Wanda asked. "I mean, if you were a widow suddenly."

"I've been a widow for years," I said. My voice was so bitter it shocked me.

"We mean a literal widow," Martha said.

"A rich widow or a poor widow?" I asked.

"Yourself—as a widow," Martha insisted.

"I'd move."

"Where?"

"Out of the West probably. Someplace warmer. And friendlier."

"She'd move back to the South," Martha said. "Once a Southerner, always a Southerner."

"What does that mean?" I said.

"No offense," Martha said. "It's just that over the years Jeff and I have found that Southerners don't adjust well outside the South, you know. They're always sort of longing to go home and you know, eat biscuits and grits and all that. Southerners just love the South—and they never quite seem to get over it. Especially college football people. Like Jeff says, 'When a Southerner talks about higher education, he's really talking about the football team.'"

"I'm going to order more wine," Wanda said. "How about you two?"

"I'm driving," I said, "or else I'd order enough wine to sink a ship."

"I'll order a bottle," Wanda said. "The you two can have some if you want some."

"I don't drink," Martha said.

"But you definitely should," I said.

"What does that mean?" She glared at me.

"It means, even the moral police have to take a time-out now and then."

"You're mad because I called you a Southerner?"

"I *am* a Southerner. Thank God."

"See, that's exactly what I mean. Do you ever hear Wanda and me say, 'We're from California—thank God'? No. We don't say that. We try to be citizens of the world."

"Give me a break," I said. I stabbed into my plate of pasta and began to twirl my fork like crazy. If you have to be rude to be a citizen of the world, I thought, then I'll pass. No, I thought, I can be a citizen of the world too. "Citizen of the world, my hind foot," I said.

Wanda laughed. "I love those Southern expressions," she said. "Really. I used to love *Hee Haw* when it was on. I'm serious. I was probably the only person in L.A. tuning in to *Hee Haw* every week."

"No doubt," Martha said.

"Too bad you didn't tune in, Martha," I said. "You might have learned something."

"Are all Southerners this oversensitive?" Martha said.

"Are all Californians this *in*sensitive?" I said.

Wanda cleared her throat as a way of declaring a truce. "You haven't told us what you would do if you were a widow, Cada," Wanda insisted. "I'm interested."

"I don't know," I said.

"You must have some idea." Martha glared at me. "We're not going to hold you to it, Cada. We're not going to make you prove it. Just imagine. You can at least imagine it, can't you?"

"Would you look for another man?" Wanda asked. "Would you try to get married again?"

"No," I said. "Will you?"

"God, no," Wanda said. "I can't even think about that yet. But they say when happily married people lose their spouses they always want to remarry—because their first spouse taught them that marriage was a good and happy thing."

"What do you think the married actor will do when he hears that Harold is dead?" I asked.

"He'll go through all the appropriate motions," Wanda said.

"Oh." I smiled. "A man who knows how to do."

"Right." She lifted her glass and winked at me. "Maybe he'll try to start things up again. I don't know."

"Will you let him start things up again?"

"Not unless I'm so lonely I've lost my mind."

"Do you think that's possible?" I said. "To be so lonely you start to lose your mind?"

"Of course," Martha said. "Where do you think art comes from? Lots of artists are so lonely they seem insane to the rest of us—and they try to make some artificial world for themselves which is less lonely and that's what art is—their attempt to connect. That's why when I go to museums I nearly always cry."

"I didn't know that," I said. "That you cry."

"I can look at all the beauty and strangeness and pain and I don't know—I start to feel so blessed myself, and so, I just cry. Jeff thinks I'm nuts."

Martha studied art in college. She has never gotten over it either.

"This is terrible to say"—I looked first at Martha and then at Wanda—"but I think I'm the tiniest bit jealous of you, Wanda."

"My God, why?"

"It's awful, I know. I hate it. But, on some level, it's true."

"I know what you mean," Martha said. "It's the freedom, I guess. It's all the possibility that lies ahead."

"You two don't have possibility lying ahead?" Wanda said. She poured wine into Martha's and my glass and we both drank it. "You think your husbands have to die so you can have possibilities?"

"You make it sound awful," I said.

"I don't wish for Jeff to die," Martha said. "Let me make that perfectly clear."

"Or Brother either," I said. "It's just that sometimes it seems like only one of us can be really alive at any given time. Either it's his turn or it's my turn, you know. And mostly it's his turn."

"Brother is a nice guy," Martha said to Wanda. "Very down-to-earth. You'll meet him Saturday after the game. I'll introduce you."

"Great," Wanda said.

"Let's hope it will be after a win too." Martha looked at me and smiled. "Right, Cada?"

ON THE RIDE home Wanda slept in the back seat with Harold's ashes hugged to her chest. His paper sack was crumpled and battered and his box was crushed and bent, but his name was still in place and easy to read: SHAPIRO, HAROLD T.

In the front seat Martha slept with her face against the icy window. She'd had four glasses of wine at lunch—probably her world's record—and now was sleeping off her sin. I was glad. Like I have heard exhausted mothers say about their problem children, I liked Martha best when she was asleep. Maybe I liked myself best when I was asleep too—maybe that was what was wrong.

I didn't take my eyes off the road the whole way home. I drove with both hands on the wheel. I knew this was a day I would need to remember. When I got home I would look to see what the date was and write it down someplace so I could remember it. Ordinarily I never knew the official date of any day. I didn't operate according to the twelve-month calendar, the days of the week, or the law of the clock. I lived in the loose seasons that made up football time. In the fall the weeks were divided into games. It might be the week of the Colorado game or the week of the El Paso game, like that. The only numbers that mattered would be the final scores. After *the season,* as it is commonly known, would come an equally intense recruiting season that would lead up to a cataclysmic signing date; then came the winter workout and weight programs and after that the fresh-breath-of-spring practice. When school was out there was another summer weight program and weeks of football camps for high school boys. Then in late July the freshmen reported to campus, and by late August *the season* started all over again. I lived my life according to this football time line—only I added my own personal menstrual cycle to the complexity of it all. Time that ticked away second by second, minute by minute, was real to me only during games. And even then it paused for commercial interruption and for the issuance of penalties and punishments. That's how football time is—fifteen seconds on the clock can translate into what seems like half a lifetime and what somebody's watch might say was twenty real minutes. Time is either too much or too little, if you ask me. Time was not the exact thing that all my life people have tried to tell me it is. Some people say time is money, but I've personally never found that to be true. Maybe time was what you made of it. And in my case that wasn't much. Otherwise time was a ocean I swam in—and lately I'd spent a lot of time in over my head.

Periodically I glanced at Wanda asleep in the back seat in her coat and gloves and boots. She'd had enough wine at lunch to tranquilize a grizzly bear—I'd been amazed, watching her drink, and now was grateful, because it had put her into a deep and peaceful sleep. She was almost baby-faced, her eyes still plumped with grief, her mouth slightly opened. I hoped she was dreaming something useful, some anecdote to all this pain. I'd read where our dreams can help us untangle the psychological knots we tie ourselves up in. I hoped that was true.

I might like to be like Wanda—sleeping off an old life, forced to start a new one when I awoke. Really scared and sad, but really free. I might like to be like that.

I wished I had had a chance to know and love Harold Shapiro. If I had known how, I would have asked Wanda for a spoonful of Harold's ashes for myself. I would keep them, maybe in a small prescription container or a little Ziploc bag. I wanted some of Harold Shapiro, to have and hold. I wanted his presence to mix with my presence because I believed I would be strengthened by it. I would not eat his ashes like Wanda was thinking of doing. I didn't know him well enough for that. But I might touch my finger into them and smear him under each eye, the way football players do. It's a practical thing they do to keep the glare of the sun or lights out of their eyes—but it gives them this bruised, damaged, dangerous look. It makes them look ready for what the world—in their case, a game—has in store.

I would like Harold's ashes to touch my skin. I would like my skin to have the opportunity to absorb some of what he knew— what he knows now. Besides, I'm the one who believes in the afterlife. I'm the one who is going to be able to imagine him there, to speak to him in prayers, to report to him on the state of the world here on earth, ask for his blessings from time to time. I believe in Harold Shapiro in a way that Wanda doesn't. I don't hold it against her either. It was not her fault she wasn't trained to believe in the good life that comes after the real life. Maybe Harold didn't believe it either, but I bet about now he really wishes he did. I could help him out along those lines. And I wanted to.

But how do you ask a woman you have only recently met for some of her dead husband's ashes? How would I explain my need for them? And if, by some miracle, Wanda were to give me some, how much time would I spend wondering which part of him I had? Would I look at his ashes and wonder if they were the remains of his brain or his penis or his heart or his belly or his left elbow or his toes with the curled yellow toenails? Maybe at the mortuary they stir everything together to keep people like me from asking those very sorts of unanswerable questions. I hope so.

IT WAS DARK when I let Martha and Wanda off at Martha's house. "Come in and have a cup of coffee," Martha said. But I declined.

Wanda walked around to my side of the car and tapped on my window. "I want to thank you," she said. I opened my car door and stepped out and hugged Wanda like she was my blood sister and only today had we learned that we had the same disappointing father who'd deserted us, and who knows how many other blood sisters roaming the world as lost as we had been. "I won't forget this," Wanda said. "I won't forget you."

"Me either," I said. I kissed a tear sliding down her cheek. It tasted like the salt of the earth.

Harold was a lump crushed between the press of our breasts. He was like a heart and Wanda and I were Siamese sisters joined at his death. We both cried again for what I hoped would be the last time that day. "I love you," I said. "I really do. You're going to do fine too, in the future. I know you will."

"I love you too," Wanda said. She held up the crumbled sack that held Harold and waved it between us. "Harold would have loved you too," she said. And I believed her.

TWO DAYS LATER Northwest State beat the Gray Wolves 17–13. It was twenty-three degrees and snowing. Martha and Wanda watched the game from the warmth of the press box. They waved to me. I sat in the stands on the fifty-yard line with other brazen souls who had their own reasons for being there.

The snow was coming down and it was like *down* was echoing all around me. We were all wearing down, and watching downs, and going down, down, down. I was. The team played hard, I swear to God. They played so hard. And I went numb watching them, my heart as hard as a block of carved ice.

After the game we had to go to the gathering of boosters and trustees at Martha's house. She had a fire going in her fireplace and hot food set out on trays on her dining room table. It was a lot like Brother and I were a couple of stray cats being let into a pen of pedigreed dogs. Just because they've got fancy papers doesn't mean they aren't still dogs. It doesn't mean they don't bite anymore.

When I introduced Wanda to Brother he hugged her. She wasn't expecting it, but Brother does that, hugs women, especially when he knows they are suffering—even me. Brother knows all about certain kinds of suffering. He might be a little bit afraid of women when they are happy, but a suffering woman, well, he's at his best with suffering females. He comes from a whole family of them.

"He's so sweet," Wanda said. "I can't believe he's a football coach."

"Lots of people around here say that," I said. "They'd like him better if he carried a gun. They'd like it if he came in here shooting and mowed half the people in this room down in a spray of bullets. They'd respect him more then."

Wanda laughed. It was the first time I'd seen her laugh. "I told

Brother I was sorry about his losing the game today," she said, "and you know what he said?" Wanda looked at me, disbelieving. "He said, 'There'll be another game next week, honey. There's always next week.'"

"That's what I hate about football," I laughed, but my laugh was sour and I knew it. "That's just one more of those sports things Brother believes that isn't necessarily true," I said. "Like *When the going gets tough the tough get going* or *Winners never quit and quitters never win* or *Never say die*—oops, I'm sorry. I didn't mean to say—you know—*die.*"

"It's okay," Wanda said.

IT WAS AFTER midnight when the phone call came. It didn't surprise me a bit but it was like Brother was getting word of the death of somebody he had just seen a minute ago in the bathroom mirror and who looked to him like the picture of health.

"Damn, Jeff," I heard him say. "What the hell? I can't believe this, man. You know this is a rebuilding year."

Sometimes Brother is just too innocent to live and breathe. It seems like a miracle that he's lasted this long in this world. If his eternal innocence doesn't kill him, it's going to kill me. I pulled the covers over my head and listened to his bewilderment turn to anger. "Man, I thought we were in this together," Brother said. "You said you were going to stand with me, man."

I laughed out loud. I shook all over, shook the bed, laughing. How does Brother keep getting away with believing we are all in this together? Doesn't he know winning is what we are all in together—and losing we are each in alone.

I knew that tomorrow Martha would come by the house early. She would bring me a Bible message written on one of her personally embossed note cards. Maybe it would say, *Forgive them, Lord, they know not what they do*, or maybe it would say, *Yea, though I walk through the valley of the shadow of death, I will fear no evil* or maybe it would say *Cleanliness is next to godliness*, which I know for a fact is not true, and is not even in the Bible at all— but, in Martha's case, I wouldn't put it past her to try and make us believe it.

# WHY RICHARD CAN'T

THERE WERE ENDLESS good reasons. For months now, Richard had lain in bed running over the list in his head, adding to it as though the reasons were dollars and he were wisely depositing them in a savings account.

*First of all, Mona was twelve years younger than he was.* This is where he began each night. He lay on his back, legs spread, hands folded behind his head, staring at the ceiling fan. The woman is thirty-six years old, he thought. In the dark she looks younger. When Richard was sixty-one Mona would still be in her forties. He shuddered.

Granted, there was something to be said for younger women, their musculature, the way coeds bolted across campus with a mix of hurriedness and forever in their gait. There was something to be said for firm breasts and shiny hair and mouths that had not said everything already or been kissed enough for the thrill to be gone from it. Richard noticed these things. He wasn't dead. He was sensible. He didn't want to attach himself to some younger woman who would remind him constantly that he was aging. "Good Lord, Richard," Mona said, "I'm thirty-six years old. Nobody can accuse you of robbing the cradle."

Sometimes Mona wasn't sensitive to the point he was making.

*Number two: Mona had children.* Richard had never had children of his own and the truth was they scared him. He didn't know how to talk to them. He couldn't tell what they were thinking. And Mona's children were girls. Two teenaged girls. My God, he must be crazy. What would it be to live in a house full of Tampax and telephone calls, and bare-legged females walking around in toenail polish and T-shirts? He supposed there must be a great deal of crying in a house full of women, and giggling too. He feared *he* might become the source of their private jokes and not know it, that laughter would gush from Mona and her daughters like a kind of sympathy.

Oh, the reasons were endless. It made no sense to dwell on it night after night. *Why I Can't Marry Mona. She is not my type, really. She expects things from me that I almost certainly cannot deliver. She thinks I am a better man than I am. She chews gum all the time — sometimes kisses me with gum in her mouth. Her divorce has made a mess of her — she doesn't know her own head yet. She couldn't possibly marry me until she finds herself.* That sounded right, didn't it? Did women still "find themselves" in the nineties? Did they still lose themselves in the men they married? Richard didn't know. He knew Mona looked at him with more sting than any woman ever had.

Mona had been in his graduate American Lit. class for almost six weeks when it occurred to Richard, much to his horror, that he loved her. She sat in the back, listening, amused. He measured the success of his lectures against her response to them. He couldn't seem to make her understand the magnificence of artistic suffering. A great artist must suffer, he told her, but he couldn't make her feel it. She said she thought *Moby-Dick* was boring. Boring. She said it was a man's story and didn't particularly interest her. Chasing a whale is a small thing, she said, compared with raising children. Chasing a whale is a luxury. Richard had never heard anything so ignorant in his whole life. She had gone on to say that Thoreau was self-reverent, not self-reliant. She said a life separate from others, untangled, unanchored, uncommitted, is the life of a coward.

"I'm not impressed by a man sitting out in the woods all alone thinking grand thoughts," she said. "Who couldn't have a lofty thought or two with all that leisure time on his hands? Who did Thoreau ever look out for other than himself? If he'd raised children on Walden Pond, fed them, clothed them, educated them, while thinking his thoughts, then that would be something. Of course, if he'd had children to raise he wouldn't have had time to think so much . . . unless, of course, he'd had a wife—"

"What kind of convoluted reason is that?" Richard had practically shouted at Mona. "There is more to life than raising children, Ms. Montgomery."

"Particularly if you don't have any," she said in a voice that embarrassed him, making him feel limited—and furious.

Mona had gone on to write a long paper on why Mark Twain was a sexy writer and Melville was an intellectual one. She said intelligence was sexy, but intellectualism was not. The woman didn't know what the hell she was talking about. But the younger students, particularly the male students, stared at her when she spoke in class. They radiated a peculiar affection for Mona that Richard found disturbing. Mona was too old for the young men in American Lit. What did they know about pleasing a woman with two teenaged daughters and absurd literary opinions? Mona had wisps of gray in her hair, he hoped they noticed that. She was out of style, dated, had not read the classics, yet he heard girls invite her to lunch after class and young men offer to buy her a beer. And before he knew what he was doing, in a stupid moment after one particularly painful class in which she had denounced the American literary canon as "offensively male," Richard had asked Mona to go for coffee. It seemed important to him that she understand. "*Moby-Dick* is the greatest book ever written," Richard insisted, "with the possible exception of the Bible."

"Bullshit."

"But the power of his vision—"

"It's a small, limited vision," Mona replied. "It excludes well over half the people populating this earth. A man who doesn't know anything at all about women just isn't very interesting, Richard. I'm sorry."

Richard was stupefied by her certainty. He couldn't decide whether to be angry or amused.

Mona smiled. "And he's god-awful boring, Richard."

Why did everything she said feel like a personal attack on him? When Mona spoke of Melville did she really mean Richard? He thought she did. He would show her he wasn't boring. Maybe she thought she had nothing to learn from him, but he would teach her a thing or two.

They walked to a coffee shop near campus, where Mona told him about an affair she had had—the only affair of her life—with the golf pro at Brook Valley Country Club, which had made her realize how desperately she needed to divorce her husband. She said she cried for a year. She very nearly cried telling the story. Richard was terrified by her honesty. It seemed so reckless—telling the truth. "Should you be telling me this?" Richard asked. "You hardly know me. For all you know I might—"

"Blackmail me?" Mona said, taking a bite of chicken salad, her tone suggesting the absurdity of his caution. Richard couldn't take his eyes off her. He didn't dare mention Herman Melville for fear of breaking the spell. Besides, he was too nervous. He had been nervous since he first laid eyes on Mona.

*But, the reasons. Yes. Why I Can't Marry Mona. Mona watches too much TV.* It was something Richard couldn't respect. In the time Mona spent watching talk shows she could have read the *New York Times* from cover to cover.

*And she eats junk food.* When every other mother was pushing bean sprouts and skim milk on her kids, Mona was making chili dogs. "We get real hungry for a good hot dog," she said the first time she invited him to eat supper with her daughters and her. She made chili dogs with onions and poured potato chips into a bowl and served baked beans crusted with brown sugar. For dessert she scooped bowls of vanilla ice cream and poured Hershey's chocolate syrup over them.

"This is Dr. Petreman," Mona had said when Richard arrived at the door carrying an eighteen-dollar bottle of wine like a carryover from some earlier civilization, "my English professor. I've told you about him."

Her daughters smiled and looked him over carefully. He felt like a foreigner who didn't understand the language. Mona's daughters asked him questions. He did his best to answer them. Yes, the fraternity parties are said to be wild. Yes, he supposed there were lots of cute guys at the university. Mona's daughters named every boy they could think of who had gone to the university, hoping maybe Richard had taught one of them—but he never had. He felt like a disappointment, but the girls smiled, saying, "You're lucky, they're Neanderthals anyway," and they giggled and continued their gentle and curious interrogation. No, he had missed the Pro-Choice march. No, he did not attend the Take Back the Night rally. Suddenly he wanted to apologize for that. He looked at Mona's two slender, dark-eyed daughters, both of them with curly hair like their mother, the younger one wearing braces, the older one wearing earrings made of feathers, and he wanted to apologize for the fact that men anywhere ever attacked women, or raped them, or beat them up, or said hateful things.

They were lovely girls, he thought, Mona's daughters. But what could they expect from life? Their knowledge of world issues came largely from television. They couldn't believe Richard had never watched a single hour of *Oprah Winfrey*. "You're kidding?" they kept saying. "You don't know what you're missing." That was exactly the feeling Richard had when he left Mona's house that night to go home.

*Love is not reason enough to marry someone.* Richard knew this. *Great sex is not reason enough either.* Even together the two are not enough. Mona had reduced Richard to a teenager. He had erections talking to her on the phone. She could not stop by his office without his wanting to kiss her and unbutton her blouse. The first time they made love he had nearly cried from the intensity of it. It was as though Mona had dismantled him, loved him in fragments, then reassembled him into an entirely new man.

When she clung to him in the darkness, saying his name over and over, climbing him and then flying from him, falling, floating, moaning, he held her as though she were his own life come loose from him. He tried to press himself through her skin and make himself a permanent place inside her. He had gone crazy, he was sure. But the only time he clearly recognized his own existence and believed there was good reason for it was when Mona called his name. "Richard," she whispered. "Richard, Richard, Richard . . ."

There were so many good reasons why he couldn't marry Mona. *For one thing, he was not absolutely sure Mona wanted to marry him.* She had never said so. Sometimes she said, "If we lived together, Richard, we could rent black-and-white movies and watch them in our pajamas. We could have dinner parties and invite only the people we like best. We could make love in every room of the house . . ." But Mona never said, "If we were married . . ."

"I HATE THE word *wife,*" Mona said. "It's such an exhausting word."

"It doesn't have to be exhausting," Richard said.

"How do you know? Have you ever been a wife?"

"You don't have to yield to the definition of the word," Richard said. "You can redefine it, Mona."

"All I know is wives are women men are stuck with. Lovers are women men choose. I prefer being chosen."

This conversation made Richard particularly miserable.

IT WASN'T THAT women were some entirely new experience for him. Richard was a handsome man who had been told so often enough. He ran three miles a day and ate sensibly. He noticed women notice. He had even had involvements, but none of them had seemed worth reconstructing his life to accommodate. He had decided at one point, nearly ten years ago, to stop noticing women entirely, except in intellectual and professional circumstances. And, to tell the truth, it hadn't been that hard to do. In that time he had published three scholarly books and countless critical articles. His life was well organized and under control.

Then came Mona with her curly brown hair, little wisps of gray in it, her stinging eyes, and her crinkles of crow's feet that Richard found strangely sexy. She sat in the back of his class by the window. When she smiled her face was full of line and curve. When Richard said something that Mona found particularly absurd, she squinted at him the way a mother gazes at a child who has misunderstood something important. There was tolerance in her expression. She was so unimpressed with logic that he found her totally unnerving.

"THE NEXT YEAR I was a Rhodes scholar," Richard explained. "I studied at Oxford."

"Oh," Mona said, smiling. "I was at Oxford too. I was Ole Miss homecoming queen my sophomore year."

For one fleeting, absurd moment it had seemed to Richard that her shallow accomplishment equaled, perhaps even exceeded, his own. It seemed impossible to impress a woman who had once worn a crown and been paraded through town on an elaborate float made of pink toilet paper. He pictured Mona smiling and waving to admiring subjects who lined the streets for miles.

He would like to have believed Mona was stupid and small-minded, he would like to have dismissed her on the grounds that she was uninsightful and under-read, but instead he began to question his own worldview. How many good movies had he missed?

While Richard was reading Kant and Camus and wrestling with deconstruction Mona had been reading fairy tales to her children. She had lived a life in which, until recently, Santa Claus, the Tooth Fairy, and the Easter Bunny had all figured significantly. They were no more absurd to her than Picasso, Matisse, Faulkner. In fact, it seemed to Richard that because Mona could conduct her life as though there really were a white rabbit that delivered colored eggs on Easter morning, she could also look at Picasso's cubist women and see herself as clearly as if looking in a mirror. She looked at Matisse's voluptuous reclining women, their rooms full of color and pattern, their legs open, their heads thrown back, as if looking at photos of her sorority sisters in a college yearbook. Mona had never been to London, Rome, or Paris, but on the other hand, Richard had never been to Disney World or Yellowstone or the Grand Ole Opry.

Every morning he ordered himself to stop thinking about marrying Mona, to stop imagining what their life together might be like. And every night he began counting again. One night he had counted up thirty-four very convincing reasons *Why I Can't Marry Mona.* He lay in bed with tears in his eyes thinking of the reasons, particularly reason number thirty-four, a reason that had twisted like a knife in his belly. Richard could not marry Mona because—oh, it was a hateful fact, the undoing of which would be no less agonizing than undoing his birth to a particular pair of parents, or undoing his age, or the color of his eyes. Richard could not marry Mona because he was already married.

RICHARD TURNED TO look at the woman beside him in bed. Joanna was asleep, her mouth open slightly, her short gray hair in place. It amazed Richard the way Joanna slept so neatly that when she awoke in the morning her hair was unmussed. She could get dressed and go off to her job at the bank without combing it at all if she wished. He had learned to admire her absence of vanity, the fact that she did not color her hair to hid the gray the way so many women her age did, the fact that she wore her hair in an efficient haircut. She was the most sensible woman he had ever encountered, and he had admired that about her almost from the beginning. She had expected very little of him during their twenty-seven-year marriage, because she understood, Richard believed, the importance of his academic work, the fact that he had needed large amounts of time alone, undistracted by the details of everyday life. She had never allowed domesticity to suck energy from his intellectual life. No children. No pets. No wife in an apron anxiously waiting for him to come home. For much of their married life Joanna had earned the larger income. She had always managed their money and made their investment decisions and deserved full credit for the fact that at this point in their lives they were financially secure— even prosperous.

Over the years Richard and Joanna had developed an understanding. She had overlooked his few indiscretions that had come to her attention. Their second year of marriage he had forgiven her for cutting her nearly waist-length hair, which she had always worn parted in the middle and hanging straight down her back. Often while sitting in the sun to let it dry, she would brush the tangles from it and it would fly from her head, full of electricity. Then one Friday afternoon Richard came home and found Joanna standing in the kitchen, pleased, not more than three inches of hair anywhere on her head. "What do you think?" she said.

This was first of many opportunities Richard had missed to tell Joanna what he really thought. "Why did you do it?" he asked.

She smiled and hugged him. "You are looking at the new assistant corporate loan officer of People's National Bank!" The following morning she went to work wearing a new gray wool suit—the sparkle in her eyes having focused. Years later Richard had had to forgive her, happily, for being a greater financial success than he was. His academic books had not sold particularly well, although one had been very generously reviewed in the *New York Times*. Joanna knew most of the worst things about

Richard's personality, as he did about hers, and those worst things had been accepted. So what if they never laughed together. Marriage wasn't a laughing matter, was it?

"MONA," RICHARD EXPLAINED. "I have been married to the same woman for twenty-seven years. How many men do you know who can say that? How many men do you know who have managed to hold on for so long?"

She had looked at him with her squinting eyes and said, "Yes, Richard, but are you happy? Do you love your wife?"

As she so often did, Mona missed the point entirely. Richard found her exasperating. She had divorced her husband because, she explained, "We weren't happy anymore and lost our hope of ever being happy together again." She said this as if it were some kind of reason. When Richard asked Mona for a further explanation, she touched his face softly and shook her head. "Life is short, Richard," she said. "Don't you understand?"

More than once Richard decided never to see Mona again. More than once he announced his intention to her. "Mona, there are too many reasons why this will never work. I've been a married man more than half my life. My father was married sixty-three years. It's a point of honor, staying married until the end, not giving up. Marriage runs in my family, Mona. Petreman men get married for life."

Mona smiled at Richard as though he were saying exactly the opposite of what he was actually saying. "Do you know what I hope?" Mona said. "I hope that when you get to heaven God will be well pleased. I hope he will give you a prize—a blue ribbon maybe—and let you wear it all through eternity. He will say over the loudspeaker of heaven, 'Honor this man. He lived all of his life with a woman he didn't love. He resisted happiness when it presented itself. He lived his life as though it were a punishment. Give this man a pair of wings. He is a saint! He is—' "

Before Mona finished speaking Richard pulled her to him and began kissing her angrily, as though he were trying to drink up the words she had spoken. "Damn you, Mona," he whispered. He locked the door and made love to Mona in his office in the English building. The world of academia traveled the halls outside, students coming and going, professors thinking, the cleaning lady sweeping. Afterward he held her, her wild, curly hair a mess, her body bearing its history, a history that seemed to him, at the moment, more important than the history of the civilized world. He ached over the fact that she had lived thirty-six basically satisfactory years without him. They lay on the floor of his carpeted office. Twice she pulled away from him to stand up and get dressed. Both times he refused to let her go. "Stay a little longer," he whispered, "please."

That night he called her and said, "Mona, this is Richard." His voice was formal and businesslike. "I am calling to let you know that I cannot possibly continue to see you. I hope you will understand and forgive me."

"I'm sure that is a very wise decision," Mona said after a moment of silence.

A week later Richard invited Mona to travel with him to a literary conference in St. Louis, where he was presenting a paper titled "Thoreau: Self-Reliance or Self-Reverence?" Mona read the title and was very moved. She said yes, she would love to spend a week with him in St. Louis.

What she didn't know was that Richard had decided to tell her once and for all that their relationship must end. He had never wanted less to do anything in his life, but he had to do it or go mad. He couldn't spend another year ignoring his academic work and thinking up ways to spend time with Mona. He had become a spectacular liar in the past year. And poor Joanna accepted anything Richard said without question. He must put a stop to the lying. Regain control. Get back on track.

But how do you tell the woman you love that you have decided not to love her? The pleasures of the trip, he hoped, would help soften the blow. He wouldn't break the news to Mona until the very last day. Until then, they could just continue to love each other and be happy.

Mona made arrangements for her daughters to stay with their father and bought a wonderful black dinner dress, two silk blouses, and a nightgown the color of peach sherbet, all of which she showed Richard, stopping by his office, flushed with excitement, on her way home from the mall. This had touched Richard deeply. He knew that as a graduate student Mona could not afford such purchases.

"I charged it," she said, absolutely glowing.

Richard spent most of the day before the trip shopping for

and packing a picnic in a Styrofoam cooler. He made chicken sandwiches. He bought wine. He bought chocolate-chip cookies, and fruit, and crackers and cheese and French bread from the bakery. He remembered the corkscrew. He bought cloth napkins—a detail that surprised and pleased him. He packed carefully, including vast numbers of maps and his favorite tapes. He whistled as he loaded the car.

Determined not to spoil the trip by dwelling on the inevitable nature of his mission, Richard put telling Mona good-bye almost completely out of his mind. He felt, instead, as if it were Joanna to whom he was saying good-bye forever. As he and Mona drove out of town together, Richard felt as happy as a man who, after twenty-seven years in a dutiful marriage, had finally been proven innocent and released. As though the world had apologized to him in the form of a million-dollar check and complete freedom—both of which he would enjoy fully when he reached St. Louis. Richard held Mona's hand as they drove past the city limits sign. Then he said the most foolish thing he had ever said in his life. He said, "Mona, let's pretend we just got married and we're going to St. Louis on our honeymoon. Let's pretend we've got forever stretched out in front of us."

Mona squeezed his hand and looked at him, her face radiating a mixture of desire and suspicion. "Richard," she said smiling, "I've been pretending that all along."

They picnicked at roadside parks, fed each other bites of cheese and cracker, and kissed like lovesick teenagers. In the car they held hands, and listened to Chopin until Mona fell asleep, her head resting on Richard's shoulder. Afterward he found a country music channel, and the hopelessly sentimental lyrics revived Mona. She knew the words to every song and sang out loud. Richard even found himself quite taken by a line in a rather awful country song, "I sleep without you, but I dream about you." "That's beautiful," Richard said.

Mona told Richard stories about her children. How her youngest daughter had asked for a different pet every year, a dog, a cat, a goldfish, a hamster, a rabbit, and finally, a boa constrictor. Mona had drawn the line there. Mona saw sexual symbolism everywhere she turned, which, she explained to Richard, had to do with being a woman and having a body flooded with estrogen.

Richard laughed at the boa constrictor story. He laughed at the talk of Mona's older sister telling her that men's penises were the same size as their feet, and Mona believing it. She and her fifth-grade girlfriends had taken up asking boys what size shoe they wore—and had received the boys' hesitant answers with a mixture of curiosity and horror.

But the most amazing thing was that Richard found himself talking. It was like the cork had been gently pried loose from his bottled-up place and he was pouring out the stories of his life —letting Mona taste them, drink them, digest them. And— dammit—it didn't hurt to do it. He was talking about personal things—and it wasn't killing him. For the first time in his life, maybe, he wanted to talk. He even told Mona about his mother. It didn't hurt either. What the hell was happening?

In St. Louis Richard delivered his paper. He attended the reading of two papers where he felt obligated to make an appearance. Otherwise he hardly left the hotel room. The room was air-conditioned and the curtains drawn, simulating endless night. Richard and Mona spent days in bed, talking, laughing, making love as though sex were something terribly expensive that they had never been able to afford—until now, since in the last week they had become sudden billionaires. They ordered room service nine straight meals.

Only one night during the week did they go out for dinner, and that was so Mona's new black dress wouldn't be wasted. She bathed and put hot curlers in her hair—which startled Richard —and made up her eyes and put on perfume. With equal parts of alarm and amazement Richard watched Mona assemble herself. In the end he thought her cosmetics had done little to damage the natural blush—the glow—she had taken on during the week.

Richard insisted that he liked Mona best without makeup, "perfectly natural," he said. She laughed at him. "You only wish you liked me best that way," she said. "And it's fine if you want to pretend . . . actually, it's very sweet."

It was not until the first night of this trip that Richard had ever seen Mona with no makeup at all, fresh, wet, right out of the shower, wrapped in a faded cotton robe. Mona had been shy coming out of the bathroom. Richard lay on the bed watching the news. He stood up when Mona entered.

"Don't stare at me," she said.

"I can't help it," Richard stammered. "You look so . . ."

"Wet?"

"Wonderful." Richard knew how stupid he sounded. He knew Mona didn't believe him for a minute. "Let me look at you."

"I have to dry my hair." Mona began digging through her over-packed suitcase for the hair dryer.

"Please," he said, his voice awkward, hitting an unexpected high note.

"I don't see why . . ." Mona turned to face him, her hair in limp ringlets, her skin bare, uneven, unpinkened, her lips color-less, her eyes contracted into a smaller size. She smiled, uncon-vincingly. Richard could not take his eyes off her. "This is it," she said. "This is perfectly natural . . . just the way you like it."

Richard wanted to say that she was beautiful, because that's what a man should say, that's what a woman expects to hear. But the truth was he had no idea whether or not Mona was beautiful at this moment. He doubted it. She looked too small, like she had showered away all the adult and was standing barefoot before him, as a little girl, totally uncamouflaged. He was overcome with the desire to protect her. To throw her to the ground and wrap himself around her while fighter planes flew overhead dropping bombs all around them.

Nervously, Mona untied the sash of her bathrobe and let it fall open, not like a woman being sexy, but like a woman being brave. Her imperfect breasts, her full hips, the cesarean scar that ran down her tummy. She was all curve, and softness and strength. Her body was beautiful *because* it was battle-scarred, Richard thought. He wanted to tell her so, but couldn't. He stepped toward her, slid his hands inside her robe, and buried his face in the dampness of her neck. "Mona," he said. "You scare the hell out of me."

"That's not a very nice thing to say to a naked woman," Mona whispered.

Richard lifted her in his arms and carried her to the bed. "I feel like I'm in some goddamned movie. This is real, isn't it Mona? This is really happening?"

"It's definitely happening to me," Mona whispered.

LATER HE SAT in the bathroom and watched Mona as she dried her hair and put on makeup. "Why do you put that stuff on your eyes?"

"It's eyeliner. It makes my eyes show up."

"What about that stuff?"

"Mascara? You're kidding." Mona turned to stare at Richard. "Doesn't your wife wear any makeup?"

Richard thought for minute. "I don't know. I don't think so."

"Oh, great."

"What?"

"I find it horrifying to think your wife is so beautiful she wears no makeup at all, Richard. But I find it even more horrifying that in twenty-seven years you haven't looked closely enough to be sure."

"I don't want to talk about Joanna."

"Just one question."

"Oh, God," Richard moaned.

"Do you love her, Richard?"

Richard wanted to say "Yes, dammit, I love my wife!" He wanted to say it for Joanna's sake, who deserved at least that after all this time, and for Mona's sake, because he understood that, strangely enough, his loving Joanna would make Mona think better of him. But mostly he wished it for himself. He wished he were capable of sustained love. He wished the structure of his life were based on something more than habit. But the truth was that whatever combination of things he felt for Joanna now, it wasn't love. Mona had shown him that. "I love you, Mona," Richard said, recklessly. "That's all I know."

That night before they went to dinner Richard showered so long the hot water nearly ran out. He shaved while Mona watched, like a scene in a television advertisement. Richard took his time, shaving slowly. He put on his dark suit. Mona had never seen him in it. It was an expensive suit that often caused attractive women to smile at him and ask how tall he was.

Dinner was elegant. Dinner was outrageously expensive. But what did it matter? For Richard the evening had taken on the proportions of the last supper. He ordered more wine. He and Mona looked intently into each other's eyes, entire sentences evaporating as they were spoken. Words were reduced to accessories, intimate messages exchanged by code. It seemed to Richard that all around him people were smiling approval.

"How long can this last?" Richard asked Mona as they lay in bed later, tipsy. "How long until these feelings run out? And then what? What comes next?"

"You think we're on the fly-now-pay-later plan, don't you, Richard?" Mona asked.

"Are we?" he asked.

"I'm not," she said. "I'm on the say-yes-to-life plan."

Richard groaned.

"I know it's corny," she said. "But I've tried pretending life is a big, somber test you have to pass so you can move on to something better in the next life. But it's a crazy test, Richard. The more you don't know, the more you don't do—the better you score."

Richard rolled over and stared at the ceiling. Everything Mona said came at him like soft bullets, not because what she said was true, but because she thought it was true. That hurt just as much. That she believed he was afraid.

She never said so, but sometimes he thought he saw it in her eyes. "I never said I was a hero," Richard said.

"Heroism is not required," Mona said. "You make me happier than I've ever been in my life."

And this was the insanity of it all. Richard heard Mona's words and believed them. He knew it was the truth.

"I never believed this kind of happiness existed," he said, turning to face Mona. "I'm almost fifty years old and happiness scares me, Mona."

Mona rolled up on her elbows and smiled at Richard. "Everybody's afraid of being happy, Richard. That's why they have so many rules against it."

FOR THAT ONE week in St. Louis Richard possessed Mona. He was ashamed to think in those terms. Wasn't that what led many a man to ruin, the insatiable desire to possess a woman? The endless effort to win her, over and over again, to claim her, as one claimed a scientific discovery that would bear his name forever? Men like their names on things, inventions, diseases, bodies of land, bodies of women. Hadn't Richard wanted to make love to Mona so fiercely that she would forget all the men who had come before him and any man who might come afterward? Didn't every man want to leave his mark on the woman he loved —a tiny scar on her heart in the shape of his initials? Was Richard any different? Why did he love hearing Mona say his name in the urgent moments of her orgasm? Why did the sound of his own name—hearing Mona whisper it or shout it—please him so much?

By the end of the week in St. Louis Richard had begun to dread the return ride home. He decided to postpone telling Mona good-bye until then. Until they were practically entering the city limits of their other lives. Richard began a silent countdown. Only three more days he told himself. Just two more days.

My God, only one day left. Then he counted hours. Twenty-one hours. Twelve hours. Eight hours. He tightened himself into knots as the week came to an end.

Mona became quiet in response to Richard's moodiness. He withdrew, became sad one minute, then grabbed Mona suddenly and hugged her until she thought her bones would break. So she began to lose her balance too. She became unsure. She reached for Richard constantly, touching his face, his hands, his body— like a blind woman trying to memorize him.

On their last day in St. Louis Mona realized that she had not called her daughters all week. And Richard had not called Joanna.

Richard imagined himself sleeping in Joanna's bed when he got home. It suddenly seemed to him to be *her* bed. The entire house seemed to be *her* house. *Her* cars. *Her* furniture. *Her* bank accounts. *Her* life in which he rented a small room, a narrow side of the double bed. When had she last known that he was in bed beside her? When had she last cared? Richard could not remember the last time they made love. Why had he stopped kissing her? Why had he stopped watching her undress and lie down next to him? Why had he stopped reaching for her in the darkness? It had all ceased to occur to him years ago. Perhaps because it had ceased to occur to Joanna several years before that. She had not announced it, but it had become perfectly clear. And he had found her indifference satisfactory. A relief. Now when he walked into a room where she was undressing, or when he rolled against her in bed, he said, "Excuse me." But when, exactly, had she started sleeping with her back to him?

THE RIDE HOME from St. Louis seemed longer than it had coming. It rained. The windshield wipers slapped back and forth, but the rain was relentless, and slowed the return trip. Richard sank into a melancholy that Mona's forced cheerfulness could not lift. Five or six times he tried to launch into the exiting lines he had rehearsed so diligently: "I don't know how to tell you this, Mona."

"Try."

"I've been thinking."

"Yes."

"Maybe we should . . ."

"What?"

". . . try to . . . go to St. Louis again next year."

"WE CAN'T CONTINUE this way, Mona."

"What way?"

"This way. You know. Happy like this."

"WHAT WOULD YOU do if I said I couldn't see you anymore?"

"Are you saying that?"

"No, of course not. But what would you say if I did?"

IT WAS STUPID and useless. Richard was a coward. If he hadn't been forty-eight years old he might have done something crazy like fly to Las Vegas and get a quickie divorce and have a quickie wedding. He might just keep driving and see where they ended up, Key West maybe, or Mexico. It was too late. It was too late for everything. How had he wasted so much time?"

"Richard," Mona said, "are you okay?"

"No," he said. "And I don't want to talk about it."

When they arrived at Mona's place her ex-husband was there with the girls. He was pleasant, younger than Richard, athletic looking. He reached out to shake Richard's hand, but Richard quickly handed him Mona's suitcase, as if he misunderstood the gesture. The truth was he could not bear to shake hands with any man Mona had ever loved. Some other man unable to make Mona happy. The sight of the man made him sick. Richard was rude. He said good-bye to Mona as though he were a chaperone who had taken her on an educational field trip.

"Thank you for one of the loveliest weeks of my life," she said.

"You're quite welcome," Richard said in an official, unfamiliar voice. He sounded like an English professor.

They shook hands in the driveway. He would not let his eyes meet Mona's for fear they would betray him with sloppy emotion. She held his hand a few seconds too long, so that he had to pull away from her.

The rain was beginning to clear as Richard drove away. He saw Mona in his rearview mirror, standing in the driveway, her hair wild and frizzy from the rain.

"HOW WAS ST. Louis?" Joanna asked.

"Fine," Richard said.

"That's good." Joanna was putting on her raincoat. "There's leftover Chinese takeout in the refrigerator if you're hungry."

"I'm not hungry," Richard said.

Joanna picked up the car keys from the kitchen counter and dropped them in her purse. "I won't be late," she said. "It's Tuesday, you know." Richard nodded. On Tuesday evenings Joanna had a director's meeting at the bank.

"Did you miss me?" Richard said.

Joanna looked at him and offered a dismissive grin. She opened the closet and began looking for her umbrella.

"Answer me," Richard demanded.

"Richard, what's wrong with you?"

"I want to know if you missed me. I was gone a week, I want to know if you noticed."

"Don't shout at me. I don't know why you're acting this way, but I'm late already—"

"Don't go."

"What?"

"Skip the meeting. Stay home and talk to me."

"Have you gone crazy?"

"It's me or the bank, you choose."

"You've been drinking," Joanna said. "God, Richard, act your age. Go to bed." And before he could answer she walked out of the house and closed the door behind her.

Richard stood at the kitchen window and watched Joanna walk to the car, get in, fasten her seat belt, and back out onto the street. The sight of her leaving, driving away, disappearing around the corner, gave him an incredible feeling of freedom.

Suppose she just kept going? Suppose she never came back? For a minute the world seemed full of possibility. Richard thought of running to the phone to call Mona. "Joanna's gone forever," he would say.

But nothing like that would ever happen. Joanna would come home and he would be there when she did, tonight, and every night afterward, because, for some reason, they both wanted it that way. They had faced the disappointment that comes if a couple is together long enough—and now there was nothing more to fear. He couldn't possibly disappoint Joanna anymore than he already had, nor she him, so they were safe with each other. He didn't want to choose happiness again because he was forty-eight and too tired to work that hard at anything. He would never want to turn Mona into the woman he had turned Joanna into. That's why he stayed married to Joanna, who neither saw him, nor heard him, nor missed him when he was gone. That's why he would always stay. Not because he was afraid of happiness, but because he was afraid of the thing that comes after the happiness.

"I'll tell Mona good-bye tomorrow," Richard said out loud. "I swear to God, I'll tell her first thing tomorrow."

Richard knew that that night he would lie in bed beside Joanna constructing a new, updated list: *Why I Can't Marry Mona.* My God, would he spend the rest of his life this way? What kind of man was he? What kind of life was this? He sat at the kitchen table, his face buried in his hands, and thought about Mona. Mona standing in her robe in the hotel room, her wet hair, her nervous smile. "But are you happy, Richard? Do you love your wife?" she had asked him.

Richard ran his finger over the salt and pepper shakers sitting on the kitchen table—he and Joanna had gotten them as a wedding gift, an ordinary set of green shakers with an S painted on one and a P on the other. But over the years the S and the P rubbed off. Now you couldn't tell the salt from the pepper until you shook it out on your plate. Life is so damned sad, Richard thought.

# TOTAL RECOIL

~~~~~~~~~~~~~~~~~~~~~~~~~~~~~~~~~~~~~~~~~~~

MY SECOND HUSBAND I married for his hands. I told you
that before. Because when it came to hands, he had them. Best
hands I ever knew of on a man. And he could fix anything with
them too, fix whatever there was. And me. Take those hands and
fix me when I needed fixed. And I married him over it. But you
know all that. That I am a fool for a nice pair of hands.

Sometimes I would say that what I know about men you could
pour into a thimble and it wouldn't be but half full. On other
days I know too much—more than I ever wanted to, and half of
that I don't like. So naturally I get nervous when some new man
starts to drive me crazy like this.

I start flying. That's the first sign. Like a feather in the air. I get all the way home after work and do not touch the ground a time. People have seen me do it, but all they can do is guess why. And if any of them guess right, I don't even care, because there is not a woman alive who would not want to be flying like I do, now and then, if she could.

The truth is I'm scared. But if I ever knew scared felt this good then I would have done a hundred things I didn't do all these years. Pick up snakes. Parachute out of airplanes. Go to war on the front line. All that stuff. Because scared is so excellent.

Well, first off, he does not call me. Ever. That man. Not on the phone. And I listen for the phone with that urgent feeling, you know, like when you have a baby in the house and you listen for any slight half-noise that might come from a baby's room. I'm like that about the telephone, jumpy and edgy like that and the man has never even called me the first time. It's just in my head that he might.

Some days I think that if the man doesn't go out of his way over me in some manner that I can clearly recognize, well, then what I am is in a bunch of make-believe, and there is nothing real about him or me or any of it. But I know better than that. Because if he is not real, then nothing is. Not the air we breathe, or our own mothers who are still living, or anything. Calling or not calling is nothing about real. Real is by itself, and what the man does or doesn't do can't change real. And the same with me. Real is going to do whatever it pleases, sit on the two of us like a tired, fat lady who did not see us when she squatted and who cannot get herself moved once she settles. And we are smashed almost flat sometimes, under REAL, like smothering in a dress skirt that smells like talcum powder. So I don't know what I worry about calling for.

Not just calling. But walking across the street. Riding down some elevator. A handwritten note. A knock on the door. Something out of the way. And so that's what I say about men. I don't know how they think. They are so unnatural sometimes. Because I need him to go out of his way over me more than I need food, or water, or rest. And it seems to me that he should know it. But what a man knows and what he does are separate. That's the part that mixes me up.

It gets to the point where a person cannot even read a book anymore. I'm not talking about a trashy book. Not heaving and thrusting. Just any book. Can't relax with a good book and forget, because at times like that the man gets himself into the book too. Don't ask me how. Don't ask me how a man does half of what he does. Gets his name in every paragraph in a book. So you can't even read the fool thing, can't keep on turning pages because it is so infuriating. So outrageous. Even the most harmless little paperback book in the world can hide a man, let him jump out at you when you start to read. Every word on a page like his smiling self. Pages like little hands reaching up at you. I am not making this stuff up. And don't think for a minute the man doesn't know it. He can act innocent all day long, but I am no fool about that. He knows it. Puts himself in every book I touch. And if I try to read in bed—well, it can't be done.

Do you think that just because I've been married twice I know everything? Do you think I should have learned some kind of lesson or something? Because I've got old marriage licenses like diplomas, ought to hang them on the wall like good credentials. Could point to them at crucial moments and say, "These are my qualifications." I have studied two men in detail, spent years at it. Even had their babies. Could hang up my children's birth certificates right alongside those marriage licenses, like advanced degrees. Because I ought to be an educated woman. I ought to be practically wise. But the truth is, I don't know beans about men. And every time I think I am through with them, seems like I keep signing up for one more crash course.

It's bound to be biological, because say what you want to, its not my doing. I'm not in control of it. So when a man starts to drive me crazy like this—which is just the third stupid time in my life—I just look the situation in the face and say, "This is meant to be." Because what else can a woman do?

I'm scared to death to listen to the radio. I think the man has connections at the radio stations and they only play what he wants them too. Every song like a special dedication. I have even heard him say to me, "All right, woman, now listen to this next song. I want you to pay close attention to this next song." I mean, he says it like he is the deejay or something, only nobody hears him but me. And he knows that I am weak over music. Soft for good songs. And he comes to me all day long on the radio. Rides that radio. Pours out of it, all day, all over me. I have almost drowned in the music before.

He is nothing like my first husband. You never knew my first husband because you didn't know me then. But this man is nothing like that one. My first man. Probably the same as yours, or anybody's. I try sometimes to think of what we used to talk about, at first, in the beginning. But for all I can remember we may never have said a word. I can't remember one. It didn't seem necessary then, to sit on a nice comfortable sofa and talk. Not when you got arms and legs and mouths, and toes and bellies. We just let the talking wait, because nothing else would. Until finally on down the road when there were things that needed said we didn't know how. And then everything seemed to just dry up—all those sweet, free-flowing juices. You're bound to know what I mean. After a while the juices don't pump like they did at first, need some words to get things going. And between us we didn't have a word. That's what I learned then—you've got to have some words. I try to keep that in mind.

But this man is different. (Which I know is what every woman says about every man. And I guess a woman can't be blamed for hoping.) We talk. Spent months talking before we even noticed we were talking. Just like two people. Talked about our children, and what's on TV, and what to get his wife for her birthday. (I knew you'd like that part. The part about his wife. Knew that would perk you right up.) We talked about our brothers, his and mine, both lawyers. I mean, I was the one voted most likely to succeed in high school and it's my brother that becomes the lawyer. Life is crazy like that. And we talked about our mothers. And college, which he graduated from, but I didn't. Two years of art school and then *wham*! I think I have uncovered the true meaning of life, again—a good man with a good pair of hands this time. And I married the discovery. Just like that. So we talked about that some—the way you see the world when you are young and completely blinded by love.

We talked about everything—just talked like people without bodies. Hardly with faces. Like two smiles that run into each other at lunch, over in the coffee shop. And pretty soon, those smiles get to laughing. Not giggling. Not like you and I do over every little silly thing. I mean hard laughing, where tears pour down, and you get way too loud for a public place, and your sides hurt, but you can't stop. And you don't really want to. He said somebody ought to give me a raise the way I put some laughter in a day.

And the crazy part was, I didn't think I was the funny one at all. I thought it was him. I thought he said things better than I had ever heard them in my life. I smiled because I recognized all the truth he was telling. There he was speaking my own mind, my own life, and putting it in such a way that I laughed—got started and couldn't stop. Because of the truth and how good he is with it. He said he did not remember when he last laughed like that, but I knew in my case it had to be sometime before I was even born—because I had never laughed like that in my life.

And the afternoon he said I was the best part of his day, the part he looked forward to, well, then that was the day he had eyes. A smile with some nice eyes. But that's all, I swear.

It was like a friendship started. That's possible, isn't it, a friendship? And we would look for each other at lunch sometimes and sit together. And on coffee breaks. And in the parking garage after work. Because we work for the same company, different departments, different floors, and he is in and out some, comes and goes. And I see him, of course, but don't really notice in any special way, and sometimes he walks by my desk and taps his fingers on it as he passes, so I look up, and we smile. Now, is there any harm in that?

Then one day at lunch he told me his idea for promoting a client's product—that recoilable telephone line. You know, you can walk as far away from the telephone as you want to, carrying the receiver with you, and the line just stretches and stretches, say, up to a hundred feet, then when you're finished you just push a button and the line recoils automatically, just like a vacuum cleaner plug. You've probably seen it on TV. No batteries or anything. Real good reception. No antennas poking out. And they even have this little headgear apparatus you can wear to hold the receiver in place so your hands are free. I bet you saw it advertised. They have a toll-free number you call and charge it to your Visa.

I know, I know, you're thinking who in the world wants a portable phone with a retractable phone line in this age of cordless cellular phones where you can just wander anywhere and never feel tied down. But hey, believe it or not this world is full of plenty of people who like to feel connected to something. Not everybody wants to be totally loose and unattached to anything. They've done a survey. And besides, already this Total Recoil phone is selling like hotcakes. Really. It meets a basic human need, you know. Communication and attachment all at once. I think there's a certain genius to it.

Speaking of genius, this man had a great advertising idea. He wanted to show people how much they could get done during just one average phone call using this new headgear device. Like you could wash the dishes, change a diaper, put a load of clothes in the dryer, and paint your nails—all at the same time you're talking to your mother. Something like that.

And I listened and commented because I was impressed—anybody would be. The man thinks so clearly, has such a nice approach. And later I jotted down a few things about what he told me, my own version of his idea. A rough sketch on the back of a letter from my sister. Only instead of having the woman talk to her mother on the phone, I had her doing business, you know. Like maybe she was a stockbroker working out of her home, or the president of her own small company, something like that. Something nineties. People would remember that, a woman standing barefoot at the kitchen sink, washing dishes, with spit-up on her blouse and placing an order for one hundred thousand coils of aluminum wire, or buying five thousand shares of IBM. Authority in her voice, you know. So I gave him the sketch and he liked it.

The next thing I know he requests my temporary transfer into his department and we are working on it together. See, he knows I majored in commercial art for two years—before love threw up a roadblock on my career path. And being a basically cooperative person, I married the roadblock, thinking at the time it would be, at worst, a glorious little detour, altering my direction just slightly, and maybe springboarding me into happy ever after. Shoot. So here I am, an artist at heart, working as a secretary —with full benefits—working overtime every chance I get because my children are always needing Chicken McNuggets and hundred-dollar gym shoes. I've already had two promotions since I got here, and I'm a good secretary. I am. But it's not what I was meant to be. And he is one person who just looks at me and sees that.

I knew I could take his good ideas and put them on a presentation board that would knock his socks off. So I did a couple of sketches and he noticed I was good. And the man is from Atlanta too, born and raised, he is no small-town, homegrown type. Not one of those boys that graduated from the University of Georgia and came to the city with his clothes in a hand-me-down suitcase. He thinks big—same as I dream. And all of a sudden we were a team, professionally speaking.

I don't know exactly when the man got to have legs and shoes on his feet, and arms and hands, one of which has a wedding ring on it, and when he got to have hair with gray mingled through it, and button-down-collar shirts, and the smell of aftershave lotion, and shoulders and pants that fit so nice, not too tight or anything. And I don't know when he sprouted this nice body—a nice man's body invisible to me all those months, but real now. And the person I like so much is in that body—got to deal with the body to get to the person. And I notice all this. Slowly. Maybe just a few freckles a day. An inch of skin, and an inch of fabric, but every inch nice, sort of familiar because I look at it every day. I don't mean I stare at the man and make a fool out of myself, but I just look at him. And I have to notice things whether I want to or not.

So here's my confession. The part you've been waiting for. It is not a confession they can send me to jail for. (Don't look so disappointed.) But here it is for what it's worth. When I noticed that this man came in a body, when he stopped being a person and started being a distinctly male person, a man as much as a person, and I noticed it against my will, well, then—I hate to say this part, but—I wanted him to notice that I was a woman. Okay. I said it.

*I wanted him to notice,* but for the longest time could not tell whether he did or not. Didn't know if I had sprouted a body in his eyes, the way he had in mine. Wondered if I had legs like he did. Or hands, or a neck, or hair, or even breasts. Couldn't tell if he noticed for sure, although sometimes I thought I saw his eyes on me, telescoping for a matter of seconds. Thought I saw him drift off in the pattern on my blouse or notice that little scar on my knee. But I wasn't sure—because I have never been sure about the things a man does. Not any man. So that's my confession. I wanted him to notice I was a woman—and at the time it didn't seem important whether nor not he was married, you know? It was irrelevant. Not a factor. I didn't care because the whole thing was purely experimental—and harmless. I just wanted him to respond. That's all. Like he could say, "You look nice today. Is that a new sweater?" You know what I mean? Say something. End of the experiment. Cut. Amen. I swear.

So the longer he took to notice, the more I tried to help him. (I hate myself for saying this.) But I worked at it a little, you know. Brushed hair, put clear polish on my fingernails. Wore more dresses, because I have legs in dresses and sometimes feel more womanish when I have legs. Lost seven pounds too, easy, without even trying. I could sort of feel myself looking better, and little by little he seemed to see it too, and when I thought he saw it, it made me look that much better, and the better I looked the more he noticed, and on and on. And I thought that if this kept up, before long we would both be perfectly beautiful—at least in each other's eyes. It was out of control. You're a woman, you know what I mean. Any woman does.

Men don't confess these things. Deny it even. But I think they do it too. Comb their hair. Stand up straighter. Wear blue. I told the man once that he looked nice in blue, brought out the blue in his eyes. And now he wears a blue shirt about three times a week. I mean it. Monday, Wednesday, and Friday— blue.

AND THEN . . . THINGS started to get a little physical, you know? That perfectly harmless little physical stuff that takes your breath away. Like one afternoon I got a cramp in my foot and took my shoe off in a fury because those things hurt. And I was hopping around the room, trying to walk the cramp out, limping and moaning. And before I know it, he is on his knees on the floor, got ahold of my foot, rubbing it, saying relax, he'll rub that cramp out. His hands kneading my foot, hard at first, then slow and easy. And I don't know if the man really has a touch that can get a cramp out or if the cramp was still there, but I just forgot all about it, couldn't feel it anymore. Not with his hands on my foot like that. That was the first time he ever touched me—and there was nothing to it really. But he was quiet the rest of the afternoon. And so was I.

Then once—I don't know how it happened—right in the middle of a sentence I felt it, his hand holding mine, as if neither one of us had a thing to do with it. Hands with minds of their own. (You don't have to believe it.) And I turned into a sixteen-year-old—maybe a fourteen-year-old—and it was the first time in my life any man ever held my hand. I was so awkward, talked a mile a minute and was too loud, sounded to myself like I was screaming—talking to him in some ridiculous, nervous way so he will not notice what our hands do when we are not looking. Afterwards I had to excuse myself and go to the ladies room to calm down.

Wait. It gets worse.

The day we finished the last presentation board for the Total Recoil account, I had done all the lettering by hand, and he had watched me like I was a surgeon operating on his only child. And when I finished, we both stepped back and looked at it. We knew the company would love the idea. We knew they would buy it, and in a spontaneous moment that began with him patting my back with congratulations, both of us were saying we did it, and ahead of schedule too. Then we were hugging, which is perfectly natural—only the hug got stuck. Just a little bit. Just enough to make the pulling away feel like aerobic exercise. Otherwise, it was a hug exactly like people give each other at football games when the right team scores. I mean, complete strangers hug like that sometimes, right?

That day I flew home like a bird to her nest. My heart singing like a bird does and I don't care how that sounds. The truth is corny sometimes. My children saw it, saw me fly in the house and flutter my wings all night long. It scared them and me too. And like I said, I never knew fear could be so wonderful. I am so happy and so terrified both—and it's a great mixture. The greatest. Do you hear what I'm saying?

Of course, I've told him about my husbands. Both of them, because you know what good stories those two make. But I didn't just tell him the funny stuff. Told the other too. Told the awful stuff I never tell anybody. Told him about those two months when I cried every day and even gave some thought to dying—and practically forgot my own name and everything else about myself. And about my second husband's hands. Those hands that I will spend the rest of my life trying to forget. Couldn't help but tell him, because he listened. He listened like his life depended on it.

You think you've got the man's number, don't you? Go on, say it. Say I am a fool. Say I am blind as a bat. Don't know moves when I see moves. Don't know a married man from a tomcat.

Okay, you're right, when it comes to moves and motives I am useless. Just usually expect the worst. That's my motto, "Expect the worst." But there is no worst to this, not yet. And maybe there doesn't have to be—just this one time. He is not a married man that forgets that regularly. Doesn't forget it now, either. And neither do I. I don't forget it for a minute. Believe me.

Sometimes I look at his face and see the confusion. The scared. Scared looks good on a man, you know that, and it breaks my heart. I want to apologize to him sometimes, for everything, for how happy I make him and how happy he makes me. I want to tell him I am sorry. That it was an accident and it will never happen again. I want to say forgive me for the laughing we've done —and the good talking. Sometimes I think I owe him an apology over it. And he owes me one.

I don't want to say his wife's name because you know her. So do I now. You wonder where my guilt is, don't you? Because as we both remember I have been the wife. I know the wife's part. Didn't my second husband teach me that much, the wife's part. The wake-up-sister-before-it's-too-late foolish feeling. And I never had sense enough to worry. Believed what he said because part of what he said was that he loved me. What woman doesn't believe a thing like that? What woman goes looking for trouble? Not me. So I know the wife's part. I wouldn't wish it on a dog.

She doesn't like the ad campaign for Total Recoil, his wife. She told him so. Doesn't that just kill you? She said a barefoot housewife running a business from her kitchen sink was not realistic. She said nobody would believe it. And after he told me that I could not sleep a wink for a couple of days. See, she doesn't understand. It was all I could do not to call her on the phone and explain it to her. Fantasy sells. That's it in a nutshell. Some people just get caught up in reality—they sort of start worshiping reality. Spend all their time rating TV on its reality factor when the truth is people do not turn on the TV for more reality. Fantasy. That's what people buy.

Life is short. I tell myself that. Life is short and goodness knows there is lots of hurt in it, and duty, and responsibility and disappointment. Can you deny that? Am I wrong? Life is short. So when good things happen in it—a person appears like a present with your own name on it, then what? Say "No thank you"? Say to him, "Go home to the mother of your children who you promised to love only and forever. Remember? You promised that. Twenty years ago you promised your whole life to her. So go on home and watch a little TV with the woman."

He told me once that after all these years his wife seemed like a sister to him. Loves his wife like a sister, and has to keep at it forever. Because the man promised. And he has a duty. I wonder if he can even sleep at night for thinking about how short life is. The man is supposed to say no to every good thing he feels—because he promised when he was twenty-one and wearing a flattop and Buddy Holly glasses that the eighteen-year-old girl beside him would be his only love. Until death do they part.

I haven't slept good in days. Just three more weeks and then I move back upstairs to my old job, mission accomplished for Total Recoil. I hope I can hold out until then. I hope I can keep my mouth shut and my body language silent. Lord knows, it's hard.

My head is like a slide projector, clicking on and off all night. That man. That man who will not call me on the telephone, but who jumps up from his desk when I come in the office, jumps up like he has been waiting, counting the minutes. And I believe it. The man who wears three blue shirts a week, for me. And holds my hand accidentally. And listens. And clears his throat when things get too quiet between us. And waits for me at lunch. Watches me walk, across the street, across the room. Watches me politely, as though he never meant to and plans to stop, starting tomorrow.

He carries a picture of his wife in his billfold. I have asked to see it several times just to sober myself up. I say, "John"—yes, John, so now you know—I say, "John, she is really very pretty. And she looks so sweet." But that's a lie. She just looks ordinary. And the picture is outdated. It's her college graduation picture, and she has on a white headband and her hair in a flip.

The late afternoons are getting hard at work. Five o'clock hits us like a blast from a hot furnace. I start to melt. I think of *The Wizard of Oz* when the Wicked Witch of the West just sizzles into a puddle like that, and it scares me. I am afraid of turning wicked, I am afraid of melting right before the man's eyes, so I go scurrying around gathering up my things, talking about having to hurry so I can see the last half of a Little League soccer game across town. I talk about mother things, and never, never, look him in the eye when I leave because I know yes is written all over me, but I just can't help it. "He is married," I tell myself every minute. "He is married. He is married. He is married."

He stands up at five o'clock and just watches me. He gets so quiet, his hands just limp at his side. He never knows what to do with his hands, so sometimes he picks up the paperweight and just sort of squeezes it, or sometimes he stuffs his hands in his pockets, but he is so stiff about it like his hands are suddenly too big for his pockets and won't fit. He says, "Have a good night."

"Thanks," I say. "You too."

"Not too great a night. Just a good night," he says.

I smile.

He clears his throat. "Any special plans?"

"Soccer," I say. "We play the Blessed Sacrament Tigers."

"Hope you win."

"Me too." I am hurrying so fast that I am dropping things. Any minute I think I will lift off the ground and begin to fly around the office.

"Guess I'll see you tomorrow," he says.

"Right," I say, nodding my head and walking toward the door.

"You forgot something," he says.

I look back and he is handing me the doggie bag I saved from lunch. Half a chicken salad sandwich. I take it from him like the bag is on fire and practically break into a run on my way out.

TWICE HE HAS showed up at Jason's games, just unexpectedly. I never know when he might come. He has a hard time explaining why he's there too. He doesn't even try to explain, just sits down beside me on the bleachers and says, "Who's winning?" Sometimes he buys us Cokes and we drink them fast, then shake those cold paper cups in our wet hands just to hear the ice rattle.

"I didn't know you were a sports fan," I said once.

"I am." He smiled. Then he cleared his throat and said, "There's a lot you don't know about me."

"I know," I said. "I just make up all the stuff I don't know. I just create it, you know, in my imagination. That way I don't have to ask you personal questions and you don't have to try to answer them."

He laughed. "So how's it going? My life in your imagination?"

"Fine," I said. "It's going fine."

Just then the Blessed Sacrament Tigers scored. They were just killing us. Again. I try to be a good sport. I know I'm supposed to teach my children to be graceful losers, but the truth is, I secretly want them to be graceful at things other than losing.

MOSTLY THOUGH, HE goes home to his wife. Straight home after work, straight as an arrow home, to his lifetime wife. Watches TV with her in their king-sized water bed—where I guess she helps him distinguish between what is real and what isn't. Maybe they laugh some too. Maybe he is just an all-round funny guy. A regular jokester. Who knows?

So what's the harm if the man flies me home at night? If I lie in bed reliving all the little tiny things in my slide projector head. Life is short, right? He has every right to go to a junior-high soccer game now and then if he wants to. This is still a free country, isn't it? He sits up straight. He pays attention. Just speaks to a couple of his neighbors before he leaves.

I have not taken to driving by his house at night or anything inappropriate like that—yet. I do not run into him at Kroger's. Even if I know for a fact that he's playing golf on Saturday I never give it a thought, I never think of an errand to run out near the golf course. This is not some shallow thing based on physical proximity. It's entirely a head thing. A shot of happiness, stretched as far as it can go without breaking to pieces or coming disconnected. There's no harm in having a little imagination, is there?

So shoot me.

## PRETENDING THE BED IS A RAFT

"TAKE OFF EVERYTHING but your shoes—in there." The nurse handed her a green hospital gown.

Belinda passed an old man standing in his cowboy boots, his green gown tied at the neck and hanging open so his backside was exposed. Luckily he'd kept his underpants on. If they make some people take them off they should make everybody, Belinda thought. She was so small that the gown wrapped around her nearly twice. She tied the strings into bows.

"Put all your clothes and belongings in this sack," the nurse said when she came back, "and have a seat along the wall."

There were seven folding chairs in a row. Old men took up six of them. Belinda sat in the empty chair. I am twenty-three years old, she said to herself, and they've got me in here on god-damn senior citizens' day.

"You having trouble with your bowels?" a pink-faced man asked the black man beside him.

"Stomach. All it does is whine and rumble all day."

"Me, it's my bowels. Bowel trouble."

Belinda didn't want to sit with these old men, so feeble not even half of them had their gowns tied on right. She was stark naked underneath her gown too. They shouldn't have the right to know that.

She sat looking at her fingernails. They'd always been paper-thin and so soft they broke right off if she just scratched a mosquito bite too hard. She had been meaning to get the fingernail clipper out and trim them good, but like half the things she was planning to do, she hadn't got around to it yet. It made her sick sometimes thinking about all the things she hadn't gotten around to. These men are old enough to die, she thought—but I'm only twenty-three. She began to bite the edges of her fingernails and tear them off with her teeth.

She wondered if the X ray would hurt. "Like making a movie out of an enema" was the way the doctor had described it. Did he think she was some kind of fool? Belinda's feet were sweating inside her leather-look shoes. When she got inside the X-ray room and took her shoes off her feet would smell to high heaven. Belinda looked down the row at the bare-legged men. The black man had on unlaced shoes with no socks. One man wore slippers. The little pink man next to her didn't have twelve hairs per leg and those he did have were an inch long and poked out like bent antenna wires.

"I hope to goodness I don't look as foolish as the rest of you," the man in cowboy boots said. "Not you, ma'am." He nodded to Belinda. "But don't none of us do a dress justice."

"If they'd a told me we was gon' be sitting out here in these nightgowns I'd of thought twice . . ." the black man said.

"I'd of worn better socks," said the man on the end sticking his legs out in the air to show that he was wearing mismatched socks, both white, but one with a red ring and the other with a green one.

"I ain't done nothing but sit since I got here," the black man said.

"How long you been waiting?" Belinda asked.

"Past long enough. Ain't ate a bite since Saturday."

"Naw, they don't let you eat nothing," the pink man said. "Hollow you out like a drum."

The nurse called, "Mr. Ward, Mr. Miller, Mr. Faulk, Mrs. Bedlow. Follow me to X ray." The group obeyed, single file, Mr. Faulk leading the line in his underpants and boots, which the others pretended not to notice.

All it was was a little blood, Belinda thought. She had quit worrying about blood a long time ago, three big-headed babies ago. Their heads like cannonballs the way they had blasted out of her belly, leaving her torn wide open and bleeding like rain all three times. And the doctor, a different one every delivery, just sewed her back up each time, like her body was some made-in-Japan outfit that had this one particular seam that would not hold and had to be reinforced every time she turned around.

"You're a mighty little girl to be having such a big-headed baby," the doctor had said after her first baby, as he stitched between her legs with his needle and thread.

"Big heads run in my husband's family." That was a lie because she wasn't but seventeen at the time and didn't have a husband.

"This'll fix you."

But afterward Belinda was not what she called fixed. Virgil said after the baby, Penny, was born that Belinda was about like making love to the Grand Canyon. He had nearly ripped her stitches loose because he couldn't wait much better than a dog. Wouldn't hardly give her time to catch her breath, never mind heal her stitches.

She had cried until he finally quit bothering her. Until he took up asking her every day or two, "Belinda, how them stitches doing? Them stitches heal yet?"

"Certain things take time, Virgil." Most nights she lay wide awake, trying not to cry, because she was afraid she would never again be the same as she was before.

Then once in broad daylight, midafternoon, when Penny was sleeping good and Belinda lay down on the sofa to get a nap too, Virgil asked her as serious as a preacher to let him see those stitches.

"Please, Belinda. I never seen stitches. I want to see how they do it is all."

"Virgil Bedlow, keep your nastiness to yourself."

"You act like it's unnatural. I'm practically your husband."

"Practically? That dog don't hunt, Virgil. 'Practically' don't put a ring on my finger, or give my mama a minute's peace. And 'practically' sure don't qualify you to look at my stitches."

Virgil married her not two weeks afterward. And now, two more babies later, here she was letting another doctor get his face right up between her legs and investigate the place she wouldn't even let Virgil investigate, and she called herself loving Virgil but never had met a doctor she liked much. And now in just a little while another complete stranger would be looking at her better than she had ever looked at herself. It gave her the creeps.

It made her think of the time she took that pocket mirror and locked herself in the bathroom to see if she could find out where the blood was coming from, but she had disgusted herself and quit it. Some things just have to be left to nature, she thought. But then she started hurting so bad—really bad—and she let Virgil drive her to the emergency room again. It was the third time in two months she had had an attack like this, but it was worse this time. She hurt so bad she was crying and Virgil carried her inside the hospital because she couldn't walk. That was when the doctors set up these X rays. They didn't want to since Virgil was out of work and without any insurance. But they wrote on her chart "unexplained bleeding," and told her to come back for special X rays.

Belinda thought about that a lot, the doctors writing "unexplained" as the problem. The problem was the bleeding hurt. When something hurts, you try to make it stop hurting. That's all. Explained or unexplained was beside the point. The truth was Belinda didn't know of much in this world that was explained to her satisfaction.

"Please have a seat along this wall," the nurse said. The group obeyed silently. When Mr. Faulk in cowboy boots sat in the cold chair he jumped at the touch of it against his skin. The nurse noticed this, reached over and said, "Let me tie that gown for you, Mr. Faulk."

The old man pulled back from her. "Naw," he said. "I don't like to be tied into nothing."

Belinda eyed Mr. Faulk with embarrassment. He's acting like he's at the insane asylum and his gown is a straitjacket, she thought. Maybe he thinks they're going to tie him to the X-ray table and give him shocks. Maybe he'd be better off if they did.

"Them machines can look right through clothes," pink-faced Mr. Ward said. "Isn't no need to make us undress like this because if the X-ray machine can see through skin then it can see through your clothes."

"If I'd a known that," Mr. Miller, the black man, said, "I'd of thought twice . . ."

"I'm thinking twice now," Mr. Faulk said. "All that's got me here is my doctor saying these tests might stand between me and cancer."

"If cancer don't scare you, you a fool," Mr. Miller said.

"I lost my wife to cancer two years ago," Mr. Faulk said. "I quit tobacco the day she died. I smoked and chewed for fifty-eight years, then just quit cold."

"I reckon you miss it," said Mr. Miller.

"I could of picked a worse habit," said Mr. Faulk. "My wife always said she'd rather me have a mouth full of tobacco than a mouth full of lies. She said as long as I had my lips all over a cigarette butt then maybe I wouldn't have them on no other kind of . . ." The men laughed at Mr. Faulk, who grinned, exposing his brown tobacco-stained teeth and nodded that "excuse my language" look toward Belinda. It was that fake politeness men do when they are secretly pleased with something nasty they have just got away with saying. It made Belinda sick when men acted polite like that.

Her own daddy had taught her every dirty joke he knew and never had made any kind of "excuse me" at the end. She had sat on the back porch, nights, with her daddy so drunk he couldn't tell if Belinda was herself or her mother or some woman named Rosemary. He had spent many a drunken hour trying to teach Hopeful, their spotted hound, how to two-step to "Amazing Grace." More than once Hopeful seemed to get the hang of it, at which point Belinda's daddy went crazy thinking about how rich they could get off a dancing dog like that. He got it in his mind that it was a story that should be covered by Walter Cronkite up in New York. Never mind that Belinda's mother kept telling him Walter Cronkite had gone off TV a good ten years ago and might even be dead by now. More than once he ran up a long-distance bill so bad that the phone company came out and disconnected the phone just to make a point. Belinda had always admired her daddy's enthusiasm once he got an idea in his head. She hadn't known back then that his enthusiasm was compliments of Johnnie Walker Red—and that she was watching him drink himself straight into the grave.

"I ain't ate since Saturday," Mr. Miller said.

Belinda eyed Mr. Miller, who was cold Alabama black with tiny little cotton balls of hair over his ears and around the back of his head. He was the skinniest man Belinda had ever seen.

"What X ray are you having?" Belinda asked.

"Top and bottom," he said. "They're going to look at them pictures and see what makes my stomach whine so."

"Well," Mr. Faulk said, "if it don't kill you it might do you some good."

"You ever been tested for tapeworm?" pink Mr. Ward asked. "Could be tapeworm that's keeping you from putting on weight."

"I used to be skinny," Belinda said, "before I had kids."

"You look like a kid your own self," Mr. Faulk said, "except I see that wedding ring on your finger."

"You look too little to have kids," said Mr. Miller.

"I'm twenty-three."

"How many kids you got?"

"Three."

"Three? Looks like you ain't had time to have three kids," said Mr. Miller.

"I got one six, one four, and one almost two." Belinda reached into her plastic bag and got her billfold out and showed the old men pictures of her kids, Penny, Patsy, and Lamar.

Mr. Miller looked at the round-faced, big-eyed children, the girls brown haired and the boy blond—like Virgil. "Woooo. They sure do smile," he said.

THE X RAY ITSELF didn't hurt Belinda a bit. It was all the probing and situating that came before that hurt. Once on the X-ray table Belinda kept her eyes shut the whole time, even when the doctor tried to get her to watch the TV screen hanging overhead and see for herself what he was doing. She had never in her life wanted to see her insides, much less now with all the tubes and dyes shot up inside her and twisting and swirling around. Especially not since she knew there was something wrong.

"There it is. That's what we're looking for. See it?" The doctor said to his nurse.

The nurse snapped a bunch of electronic buttons and Belinda heard the whirr of machines all around her. Then she heard the doctor saying the word *biopsy,* and the nurse scurried all over the place grabbing up metal instruments and making a squeaking sound in her rubber shoes. Belinda was trying to pray even though she couldn't remember a single time in her life when praying had ever helped anything—but still, lack of results had never stopped her from trying. All she could think of at the exact moment was "make a joyful noise unto the Lord," so she just kept saying it over and over to herself, "make a joyful noise, make a joyful noise."

VIRGIL WAS WAITING out in the car with the kids when Belinda came out after her X ray. He didn't have any better sense than to let the kids eat Dairy Queen dillies while they waited, so when Belinda got in the car she sat in a glob of cherry dilly that Lamar had spilt. Virgil started the car. Belinda kissed Lamar and handed him over the seat to his sisters.

"So," Virgil said, "what'd they say this time?"

"Mama, we're thirsty," Penny said. "Can we stop and get a Dr Pepper?"

"Y'all just had ice cream." Virgil backed the car out of the parking lot. "Lamar, you sit still, you hear me?" He swatted at the boy, who started to cry.

"See what you done?" Belinda said to Virgil.

"Stop it!" Patsy shrieked, pushing Lamar over onto Penny's lap. "He stepped on my leg, Mama! Make him move over."

"I don't want him on me." Penny shoved Lamar back onto Patsy, so Patsy and him both screamed twice as loud.

Virgil slammed on the car brakes and leaned over the seat. "Do you want me to stop this car and wear your butts out?" he shouted, red-faced. The children quieted and sat in their places, pouting.

"Patsy won't stop touching me," Penny said.

"If I hear another word I'm going to touch all three of you—with my belt," Virgil shouted. "You hear me?" The children nodded and sat wilted but quiet on the hot plastic upholstery. The truth was Virgil had never used a belt on the children. His threats always seemed to work well enough.

Virgil ran his hand through his wet hair and eased the car out into traffic. It was hot for April. They drove several blocks, Belinda holding her hand out the window, opening and closing her fist. Her fingernails were bitten to the quick and pink with soreness. She had to tell Virgil. He had every right to know. "Virgil . . ." she said, but he wasn't listening.

Two screaming fire trucks appeared in the rearview mirror. "Look out, Daddy," the children shrieked. Virgil tried frantically to maneuver the car out of their path. "Shit!" He gunned the motor and shot across two lanes of traffic. The sirens, startling and deafening, came from out of nowhere, almost sideswiping him as they roared past. Virgil ran a red light and swerved completely off the road, nearly hitting a sign that said CAUTION SOFT SHOULDER. "Damn." Virgil slammed on the brakes, sliding to a stop, slinging the children hard against the front seat. "Sons-abitches going to kill somebody." He looked at the children, stunned but unhurt, as they climbed back onto the seat and put their faces to the window to watch the fire trucks race on. Virgil flung his head back against the seat and ran his hands over his face. "Damn."

Belinda touched Virgil on the arm, and said very quietly, "They found a spot on my womb, Virgil."

THEY LIVED IN a rental trailer behind Belinda's mother's house. They had gotten a little behind on the rent—two and a half years behind to be exact—since Virgil had been out of work and just able to pick up odd jobs now and then. So in exchange for free rent Belinda and Virgil listened to Grace's endless talk of Satan. Every bad thing that happened, from the earthquake in Mexico to Lamar wetting his pants, Grace called a Satan attack.

"A spot on your womb?" Grace said. "A malignant spot? My God, Satan has outdone himself now!" She hugged Belinda fiercely, crushing her. "I rebuke you, Satan, in the name of Jesus Christ our Lord and Savior! Do you hear me down there?" She waved her arms above her head and began to cry, "Satan has given my baby girl cancer!" She shrieked upward to God and downward to the Devil, a frantic translator, her body undulating and contorting wildly for several minutes. Then she was still.

"You got to get baptized now, baby," she said, grabbing Belinda by the shoulders and squeezing. "You got to." She looked right into Belinda's eyes. "Promise me."

"I've been baptized, Mama. That time at Gulf Shores."

"That don't count. Nearly drowning yourself in the ocean is a completely different thing. Getting baptized can't be an accident.

It didn't take, baby. You know that. You're a backslider like your daddy, so you got to keep on until it takes. You got to get baptized for real."

"Maybe." Belinda looked away from her mother.

*"Maybe?"* Grace shrieked. "God hates *maybe*! He hates it worse than a flat-out no!" She circled the room with her arms raised. "Satan, I rebuke you for making my baby say *maybe* when anybody worth a damn can see it's time for her to be saying yes. Yes! Yes! Yes!"

Patsy and Penny ran from the room, and little Lamar climbed up under the coffee table and lay dead still, sucking his thumb.

"Don't start this, Mama," Belinda said, "Please."

"If you die unsaved, I'll never forgive you, baby," Grace said. "If you die without inviting Jesus into your heart . . ."

"Shut up, Grace," Virgil shrieked. Belinda and Grace both turned to look at Virgil, who had never before raised his voice at Grace, his mother-in-law, his landlady, primary authority on salvation. Virgil cleared his throat and said, "Belinda is not going to die. And that's final."

THERE ARE THINGS that take a little while to get used to. Your own death is one of them. The news hit Belinda the same way it had when she was five and her daddy, who was a preacher then—way back before he switched his allegiance from Jesus to liquor—predicted the end of the world, on March 4, 1979. Belinda had agonized for four long months until then, listening daily to her daddy's rendition of "the fiery end" and what would happen to all who were not good enough or forgiven enough to fly up to heaven with the angels. She swore it was the fear of hell that had stunted her growth. And then, March 4 comes and . . . NOTHING.

Late that night, seeing that God had let him down and that his family was alive and well whether they deserved to be or not, Belinda's daddy had sat out on the porch, finished off a whole bottle of whiskey, and cried. "A man can't count on nothing in this life," he said, "except disappointment."

"Maybe things will go better next time," she said, patting him. Belinda realized then that her daddy didn't remember that March 4 was her birthday. She had lived to be six years old and the world had not ended. God hadn't declared her birthday the worst day in the history of the world, which she appreciated. But God's failure to do so broke her daddy's heart.

So maybe the end of the world would not come this time either. The doctors had said they needed to study the X rays. They said the word *biopsy* so many times Belinda wanted to slap their faces. They said it might be possible to go in and cut away that spot, but Belinda knew better. What did they think, that people were like bananas and you could just cut off the rotten spots and everything would be fine? No. If there was a rotten spot in Belinda it was floating all through her and would not sit still long enough to be cut out. She understood that completely.

Three nights in a row when she and Virgil got into bed he did not even try to make love with her. Instead he wrapped himself around her, laid his head on her bare breasts—which suddenly felt to both of them like hard knots under her skin, all the softness gone from them—and he wept pathetically. Belinda held his head in her arms as though it were detached from the rest of him. "You haven't cried since your daddy's funeral," Virgil said to Belinda, as he sat up and wiped his eyes with the backs of his hands. "You're the one that ought to be crying."

"I'm saving it up," she said.

"It's not normal, holding things in like that."

"If I start crying, I'll never stop, Virgil. I'll flood this trailer and drown us all."

"You're going to bust wide open if you don't."

THAT NIGHT SHE dreamed Virgil's head was a football and it was her job to get it across the goal line without fumbling. She kept running in the dream, gasping for breath and gripping Virgil's head tight, pressing it against her breasts. Huge fat men were chasing her, grunting. Just one more step and she would score! Then—suddenly—the goal line disappeared. And a whole stadium full of people roared with laughter at the way she had been fooled.

She woke up because Virgil was slapping at her in his sleep, trying to get his head loose from her grip. "It's too hot to cuddle," he said, and rolled over on his side of the bed. Belinda cried most of the night, because in the dream she was humiliated in front of thousands of people.

"I always wanted to do things with my life. You know, Virgil? Something people would notice."

Virgil didn't answer.

THE THIRD NIGHT, after Virgil began to snore, Belinda got up and went to the kitchen, where she rummaged through the pot-holder drawer looking for a pack of cigarettes that her mother had left. She had never smoked, but now that she was dying she figured she might as well. She lit a cigarette on the gas stove, singeing her hair in the process. Then she climbed up on the counter and reached into the small cabinet above the refrigerator where Virgil kept his liquor. She pulled out a bottle of gin and poured herself a glass. She tore a page out of one of Penny's school notebooks, got a pencil from the rack over the telephone, and sat down at the table and spent most of the night writing a list.

THINGS TO DO BEFORE I DIE.

1. get baptized one more time
2. get my picture made the next time the photographer comes to Sears (give copies to everybody)
3. make love to at least three other men (just to see what it's like)
4. find Virgil a girlfriend (who likes kids)

5. tape record birthday messages for my kids up until they turn 21. Tell them I love you every day.
6. smoke and drink all I want to
7. cuss all I want to
8. tell the truth if I feel like it
9. lose ten pounds and get a better hairstyle

The next morning Belinda called Virgil's sister, Delores, to see if she would cut her hair and give her a body wave. Delores agreed and threw in free "sun streaking" which Belinda did not even ask for and which made her hair sort of golden around her face, almost angel-like. It took almost four hours altogether, because Delores had to work Belinda in between her regular customers. Belinda spent the extra time asking Delores about the girls Virgil used to go with before he met her. And Delores backtracked through Virgil's flimsy love life all the way to when Virgil was in the sixth grade and liked a girl named Candy, who Delores remembered as "very developed for her age."

"What ever happened to her?" Belinda asked.

"I don't know. Probably everything. Here." She handed Belinda a mirror and swung her around in the swivel chair. "See if you like your hair in the back."

Belinda studied the back of her head. She was thinking, "I've gone all through my life just fixing the front of my hair, and the sides—because that's the only part I could see. I've never worried about the back of my hair—only other people see that."

The thought seemed to prove a selfishness in her that she had always suspected was at her core.

"I like it." She handed the mirror back to Delores. Delores told Belinda that if she wanted to come back the following Thursday she would glue on some false fingernails too. And she wouldn't charge her a dime to do it either.

"Look at Mama!" Patsy shouted when Belinda came home. "She's beautiful." Virgil looked up from the newspaper and whistled.

"I want Aunt Delores to do my hair like that," Penny said.

Belinda smiled, not just because her family thought she was pretty, but because Virgil had been circling phone numbers in the jobs section of the classified ads and she had not had to say a single word to make him do it.

THAT NIGHT WHILE the family slept, Belinda smoked another cigarette and sipped another glass of gin and wrote a second list.

Virgil,
  This is what I need for the funeral.
  1. new dress (can put on layaway)
  2. matching shoes (size 5 narrow) (see if they have any real leather ones on sale)
  3. new bra (30-A, fiberfill)
  4. new bikini panties (size 4)
  5. new lace slip (size 30, girl's dept.)

6. panty hose (petite, Nearly Nude)

7. tasteful earrings (let Delores pick them out)

8. outfits for kids

9. new suit and tie (for you)

(Delores promised to fix my hair.)

(Do not let Mama talk about Satan at my funeral. It scares the kids.)

When Belinda went to bed she dreamed that the old black man from the hospital died. All the men waiting for X rays were at his funeral in their green hospital gowns, underpants, cowboy boots, and mismatched socks. They said he died of tapeworm. No, they said, he died of starvation waiting his turn to get X-rayed. When Belinda looked into the casket that the doctors were rolling up and down the hospital hall he looked like he was asleep with his skinny hands folded over his chest. He looked peaceful until Belinda noticed his feet and saw that they were burying him in those same unlaced shoes with no socks. She screamed for them to stop! She screamed that Mr. Miller wasn't ready yet . . . but nobody could hear her, not the doctors in their masks or the old men in their green gowns, which flapped in the wind like angel wings lifting them up off the ground. Belinda woke up gasping for air. She sat upright in the bed and looked over at Virgil sleeping with his mouth open.

The next morning she gave Virgil the list. "I don't want to be buried in any old stuff, Virgil. Promise me."

He looked at the list and went completely pale. He had to sit in a chair to read it all. When he finished he looked up in silence at Belinda, who was scrambling eggs for the kids' breakfast.

"I'll pick out my own dress, put it on layaway. The rest we can get little by little, but if I go before we've got it all you'll have to get the rest yourself. I wrote down all the sizes."

Virgil folded the list and put it in his shirt pocket. He ran his hand through his uncombed hair.

"Put Lamar in his high chair," Belinda said.

Virgil began stuffing the boy absentmindedly into the chair, hurting his legs. Lamar began to cry. Virgil slid back the tray and tried it again. Belinda put a plate of food in front of Lamar and he stopped crying.

As Virgil walked out the door Belinda called, "Wait, Virgil!" She was washing Lamar's face with a washcloth. "The panties and bra and slip, you know, I want them to match. Make sure. I always wanted a complete set of matching underwear."

THE HOSPITAL CALLED that afternoon because Belinda had missed another appointment. She apologized and let them reschedule her in two weeks, knowing full well she was not ever going to that hospital again unless they took her dead body there to do an autopsy.

THAT NIGHT BELINDA told Virgil she was going over to her sister's house in Moulton and instead she drove out Highway 64 to the Bare Facts Lounge. It was her sister, Lily, who had told her about the place. Belinda made sure it was a Tuesday because that was ladies' night and the drinks were free. The whole evening shouldn't cost her a penny.

On her way she stopped at the Texaco station and went in the bathroom to put on extra lipstick and tease her hair up a little bit and unbutton her blouse two buttons. She couldn't let herself die wondering whatall she had missed.

Virgil hated to dance. Belinda had not danced a single dance since she'd married Virgil. But inside the Bare Facts the music was so good she felt something stir inside her just listening to it. It was happy moaning. And it was dark inside the lounge too and she didn't know exactly what to do once she walked in, but it didn't matter because right away a man came over to her and said, "You want to dance, Sugar?" and she said yes.

He was twenty-eight, his hair was black and his name was Gable. His mama named him after she saw *Gone With the Wind*. He was a good dancer and pretty cute if you looked at him right. He had come to Alabama to work on the new interstate, was from just outside New Orleans, and liked to drink beer in long-neck bottles, which Belinda thought was classy. He told Belinda she had pretty hair and acted real interested when she showed him the pictures of her kids.

"Looks like you got a real tiger on your hands." He was looking at Penny. "And a sweet pussycat"—looking at Patsy. "And a linebacker"—looking at Lamar. "I sure hope your husband is not a linebacker?" he smiled.

Belinda laughed. "No, he played shortstop."

Gable howled, and twirled Belinda out onto the dance floor. By their third or fourth dance Belinda was not a bit nervous. When any other man asked her to dance, she smiled and said no thank you, then smiled at Gable, who winked at her. She drank three gin and tonics and by ten-thirty was thinking of some way she could get Gable to kiss her. It wasn't hard to do. When they slow danced she looked him right in the eye and smiled. Then she slid her hand down his chest and rested it lightly on his belt. (Touching Virgil's belt like this used to work with him—even if she did it accidentally.)

"Let's get some air," Gable said. And they walked outside and he started kissing her and kissing her and kissing her. Her heart was pounding just the same as it would if she loved him.

They couldn't go to Gable's place because his wife and little boy were there, and he didn't suggest a motel, which was fine with Belinda because she wouldn't go to one anyway. They drove out to the interstate construction site, a quiet dirt road that Gable knew about, and he rolled out a piece of tarp in the truck bed and they lay down together in the moonlight. Belinda had never dreamed that getting made love to would be as easy as this. She had expected to have to try harder.

"We can pretend this is the Hilton Hotel down at Daytona Beach, overlooking the ocean," Gable said. "Or the Fairmont Hotel in downtown New Orleans."

"Have you been those places?"

"Actually, no. I never have. But I been to Paradise Motor

Lodge just outside Mobile." This struck them both as hysterically funny and they lay in the truck hooting with laughter.

"It's okay," Belinda said. "I'm real good at pretending."

"Good." Gable wrapped his arms around Belinda. "I like a woman with imagination."

Gable was a good kisser. She would have been happy to lie there for hours and let him just kiss her. Virgil had forgotten all about kissing he was always in such a hurry to get to the other. But Gable went slow, which Belinda thought was nice. It gave her time to enjoy each individual aspect of things.

When Gable was naked Belinda stared at him. She asked him to stand up so she could see him better and he laughed at her, but he did it. She looked him over in a way she had never looked at Virgil and he didn't seem to mind. She was suddenly so brave. She looked at him in pure amazement. "You're beautiful," she said.

What she couldn't believe was that his, you know, penis was not at all like Virgil's. Virgil's penis was pink, so pink that it sometimes glowed in the dark. But Gable's was dark and bluish, and besides that he had lots of hair on his chest that ran down his belly pointing like an arrow. It took Belinda's breath away. She had never known men's penises came in different colors.

"My husband is the only man I've ever made love to," Belinda whispered.

Gable smiled, looking at her hair, which went a little frizzy in the damp night air. He probably thought she had naturally curly hair. And he was smart enough to know which questions not to ask. "Listen," he said quietly, "I don't want to do anything you don't want—"

"We have to!" Belinda said, louder than she meant to. Then she said softly, "I want to."

THAT NIGHT GABLE trailed Belinda all the way home to make sure she got back safe. She could hardly keep her car on the road because her mind was still in Gable's truck bed, where she had gotten so deliciously dizzy and couldn't seem to undizzy herself afterward. She had never heard a man say so many sweet things in her life. Now that she knew what words could do for making sex seem like so much more than sex she would not be the same anymore and she knew it.

She had been lying there thinking she knew why Gable's wife married him, because of all the things he could think of to say between kisses, and right in the middle of lovemaking—right in the middle of it!—Gable said, "Your husband is one lucky man, Belinda. I hope to God he knows it." After that she could not undizzy herself.

When she got home she went straight to the kitchen and got out her list from the bottom of the pot-holder drawer where she had hidden it. So far she had only checked off "get a better hairstyle." Now she checked off "smoke and drink all I want to." Then she crossed out the line that said "make love to at least three other men" and wrote above it "make love with Gable three times."

When she got into bed she looked at Virgil, asleep and clutching her pillow in such a way that she could not bear to pull it loose from him. She kissed him lightly and lay down beside him in the dark.

WEEKS LATER BELINDA was in line with Penny, Patsy, and Lamar in the Sears children's department. She was wearing a borrowed dress and her new hot pink fingernails. Delores had fixed her hair and done her makeup for the picture. She was having the kids' picture made too, because she thought it might be nice to be buried with a picture of them in her hand the way some people get buried holding little Bibles or plastic lilies.

The trouble was keeping the three of them still and quiet in the borrowed Food World buggy while they waited in line. She had already gone through one pack of breath mints trying to keep them quiet and was pulling out the sugarless gum when she heard someone behind her say, "Hey there, Candy. I heard you moved back. Sorry to hear about you and Cliff breaking up."

"Well, don't be sorry," the woman said. "I'm not."

Belinda turned to look at the woman in line behind her. She was a pretty blond woman with a huge bosom. She was wearing shorts and her legs were birdlegs, but very tan. She had no waist, but it didn't matter because her chest was what you mostly noticed. Belinda said to the woman, "I don't guess you're the same Candy that used to know Virgil Bedlow in the sixth grade?"

The woman smiled. "Sure, I knew Virgil. Skinny boy with blond hair."

"Right. He's my husband now."

"Oh, that's nice."

"I couldn't help overhearing that you're divorced."

"Yes." Candy rolled her eyes and took a cigarette out of her purse. "Thank God."

"Smoking is bad for you," Penny said.

"Hush, Penny." Belinda put her hand over the child's mouth. "I was thinking," Belinda said, "Virgil would love to see you again. Why don't you come by the house sometime."

The woman stared at Belinda suspiciously. "I haven't seen Virgil in ten years. I wouldn't know him if I saw him."

"He looks good. He hasn't got fat."

"Why do you want me to see Virgil so bad? You don't even know me."

"I've heard Virgil mention you," Belinda lied, but she could see Candy didn't believe her.

"You do like kids, don't you?"

"Sure."

"You got any kids?"

"One. Toby. He's five. He's living with his daddy right now."

"I see," Belinda said.

Candy sucked hard on her cigarette, her hand shaking a bit. Belinda could see that Toby was the subject that could unravel Candy and she was touched to know it. And Virgil would go crazy over a huge set of bosoms like Candy had underneath her mint green stretch top. Belinda could forgive another woman huge breasts if she had reason to believe there was a heart of gold underneath them.

"So you'll come by and see Virgil?"

"No, I don't think so."

"Next!" the photographer said, motioning to Belinda and her kids.

"Look," Belinda said to Candy as she lifted the kids from the grocery cart and herded them over to the carpeted box in front of the camera. "You want to know the truth? I've got a spot on my womb. I could die anytime and when I do Virgil will be real lonely. And from the sounds of it, you're pretty lonely right now too . . . and I just thought . . . well . . . the two of you might—"

"Our turn, Mama!" Penny pulled Belinda away. Belinda posed for her own picture while the kids stood beside the photographer saying, "Smile, Mama. Say 'cheese.'" Belinda licked her lips till they shone and grinned, showing her teeth.

Afterward, as Candy took her own turn in front of the camera, she said, "You tell Virgil I said long time no see." So Belinda wrote their address on the back of a two-for-the-price-of-one Safeguard soap coupon. "In case you want to come by sometime," she said. Candy took the address, folded it, and stuck it inside her knit top. Belinda imagined Virgil's home address resting in Candy's cleavage. She herded the kids through the Sears store and out into the afternoon heat.

On the way to the car she spotted old Mr. Faulk walking along

with a lady friend, a short fat woman. Belinda almost didn't recognize him with his clothes on, a snap-up cowboy shirt and a pair
of black polyester jeans. And he was wearing a cowboy hat and
sunglasses and chewing on a toothpick. It was his boots that gave
him away.

"Hey," Belinda said. "You remember me from the hospital?
How did your X rays come out?"

Mr. Faulk recognized Belinda, looked at the grocery cart full
of kids, and smiled. "Diverticulitis is all. You know, when your
intestines balloon out and you get these little pockets of waste
that you can't pass, and—"

"I don't want you to tell me about it."

"They got me eating oats three times a day. I feel like a horse,
all the oats I eat."

"It could of been worse," the fat woman said.

"How about you?" Mr. Faulk watched Belinda move away, the
cart rattling on the gravel.

"I got bad news," Belinda shouted.

WHEN BELINDA GOT home Virgil was furious. His red face sent
the kids scurrying to the back of the trailer. "What the hell do
you think you're doing?" Virgil grabbed Belinda and shook her as
he spoke.

At first she thought he must have found out about Gable, but
she didn't see how. They had been really careful, only seeing
each other at the Bare Facts Lounge the last five Tuesday nights

and a couple of afternoons at her sister's house when they thought Lily would not be home. Once she had walked in on them. They had already made love and were making cheese and pineapple sandwiches in the kitchen. Lily had stared at them a full minute before thinking of what to say. "Belinda Bedlow, Virgil is going to kill you!" Belinda smiled and sat on Gable's lap. He was wearing nothing but his underpants and was very embarrassed. "I'm going to die someday anyway," she answered.

"The hospital called!" Virgil shrieked. "And your doctor called! They want to know what's wrong with you!"

"I thought it was their job to know."

"They say you haven't been showing up for your appointments. They say you don't return their calls." Virgil's face was anguished.

"That's right."

"Shit, Belinda, don't worry about paying for it if that's it. I'll get—"

"It's not the money." Belinda slung a Sears bag into the closet.

"What then?"

"I don't want any treatments."

"You don't want them?" Virgil slapped his hands against his head. "They said you might die without the treatments, Belinda."

"They never said these 'treatments' could keep me from dying. It'll kill me faster, Virgil. Don't ask me how I know, but I do. Besides, all my hair will fall out and—"

"Your hair?" Virgil sank into a chair and looked at Belinda like she was a total stranger.

"It'll kill me faster, Virgil. I can feel it."

"So." Virgil stood up, began pacing around the room. "My wife has cancer and that's just fine with her, right?" He picked up a pack of cigarettes from the kitchen table, where Belinda had left them the night before, and slung them at her, hitting her in the chest. "You know what I think? I think you want to die, damn you."

Virgil grabbed the car keys and two beers, hung together in their plastic noose.

"Where are you going?" Belinda said.

"I'm getting out of this insane asylum."

"I'm the one dying," Belinda shouted. "Or have you forgotten?"

"Well, I don't have to hang around here and watch you enjoy it." Virgil walked out the door.

Belinda picked up the closest thing, an open jar of strawberry jelly sitting on the kitchen counter, and threw it at Virgil just as he shut the door. The jar hit the door and broke. Sticky, red goo splattered everywhere. "I hate you," she said.

SOMETIME AFTER MIDNIGHT Virgil came home drunk. The kids were asleep. Belinda was sitting at the kitchen table reading the instructions for the new tape recorder she had charged at Sears on her mother's credit card. Virgil stumbled over to her and she stood up to help keep him from falling. He put his arm around her and she walked him back to the bedroom, where she pulled off his boots and helped him into bed.

"Virgil," she said, "I didn't really mean it when I said I hated you."

"I know that. You married me, didn't you?" He rolled over on his back and crossed his arms over his forehead.

"I'm just so tired, Virgil, you know? And if I have to die I want to do it right. That's all. I want to do dying better—Virgil, are you listening?"

Virgil was sound asleep with a smile on his face.

BELINDA SAT UP most of the night talking into her new tape recorder. She made each of her children four years' worth of birthday messages that first night, and kept it up over the next few weeks until she had them all legally grown.

Penny,

I bet you're real pretty now. You'll have to ask your daddy to explain things. He won't want to talk about it, but keep asking him. He knows even if he acts like he doesn't. If your daddy has a new wife, then ask her instead. Women always know more about the facts of life because most of the facts happen to women. I love you.

Patsy,

When I was eight it seemed like Lily had a better time of things than I did. Her being the oldest sort of smashed me down. So don't let that happen to you. Sometimes your daddy might try to speed you up to Penny's age and sometimes he might try to slow you down to Lamar's age, but it's just because you're in the middle which gets him confused. Mama loves you.

Lamar,

If it seems like you get yelled at more than anybody and blamed for everything, it's just because you're the youngest. One day you'll probably be bigger than everybody in the house, even your daddy, maybe. If you have a new mama now I hope you like her. It won't hurt my feelings. Love, Mama.

Then Belinda made Virgil a couple of Christmas messages.

Hello there.

Just be careful, Virgil, picking out a new wife if you haven't done it already. You have to pay close attention to what you're doing the second time around.

Virgil,

This is the last Christmas message I'll make since you're surely remarried by now to a woman who probably won't want to hear your dead wife's voice wishing you a Merry Christmas on a tape recorder. I bet you've forgot all about me by now. But don't admit it, if you have. Do you ever think about that night at Elk River?

And she even made her mama a couple of Christmas messages, too.

Mama,

Guess what? I'm up in heaven and—I know you won't believe this—but Daddy is up here too. God is so much better than you ever thought. He forgives people.

Mama,

Merry Christmas again! Me and Daddy are having a great time flying around up here. You can see everything from heaven. Sometimes for fun we fly over New York City and hover around watching all the Yankees and foreigners. You are right about New York City, Mama. It is every bit like you imagined and me and Daddy think it's probably the best thing that you live in Alabama.

Happy New Year!

Making the messages was exhausting, but Belinda went about it in a very organized manner. As soon as she got them all finished she was going to give them to a lawyer that Dolores's husband, Kicker, told her about who could dole them out one message at a time on the proper dates. She had handwritten all the instructions and dates for the lawyer so nothing could go wrong. She couldn't leave the tapes with Virgil. He would listen to all of them the first night and after that he might lose them altogether. Same with her mama and Lily. So a lawyer was best. She had never met any lawyers, but she loved the idea of having a professional handle things in her absence.

GABLE WAS ON Belinda's mind twenty-three hours a day now, leaving only one hour to cram everything else into. The only way in the world I can give him up is to die, Belinda thought. He was like medicine—that tasted good. A painkiller she was addicted to.

Belinda thought heaven must be a place full of men like Gable. Enough to go around. One for every woman. Men with lips like a bed you lie down in. Men who know the things to say that Gable knew. His mouth. It kissed her, it spoke to her, and it could do other amazing things that caused her to come out of her skin and rise glimmering and fluttering like some powdered moth toward a hot light overhead. He could make her moan and scream and afterward he could make her laugh. It was worth dying young for.

Gable didn't know Belinda was dying and she never wanted him to. She liked how it was between them and didn't want to mess it up with sympathy. One night they were wrapped around each other, naked, late, late at night, the rain falling warm and sweet and before she knew it Belinda was saying, "Gable, I love you. I love you." The words came out of her in abrupt uncontrollable leaps, like burps, burps she felt rise up from deep inside her, slide up through her chest, puffing as they went, until finally, they surfaced and blurted out. "I love you," she kept saying and Gable hugged her so hard she thought she would break in half.

"Baby," he said. "Sweet, sweet Baby."

Belinda burst into tears and clung to him, wrapping her bare legs around his, her arms tight around his neck. She buried her face in his chest and cried the way a car moves with its tires flat, a slow, powerless thumping, a lopsidedness, that must run its course before the brakes can be applied. Gable rocked her back and forth. But she couldn't stop crying. "You cry all you want to, baby," he said. And she did. She cried like she was breaking and crumbling into tiny parts inside and crying herself out in lumps. He kissed the top of her head and kept rocking her and rocking her. "I'll help you, baby," he whispered. "Whatever it is, I'll help you."

When she awoke the wet tarp was pulled over them and the rain had stopped. She thought at first that Gable was asleep too, but when she lifted her head she saw that he was watching her. As soon as she stirred, he reached for her, tucked her hair behind her ears with his warm hands, pulled her close, and whispered sweet things.

Afterward she went home to limp-limbed Virgil, sprawled half on and half off the bed, exhausted from his halfhearted job search, asleep with the TV on. She looked at him as though he were one more of her children, a sweet boy someone must take care of. She brushed the hair out of his eyes and turned off the TV and turned off the lights and climbed into bed beside him, thinking their bed had the hardest mattress in the world, amazed that a tarp-covered metal truck bed could seem so much softer and warmer, even in the pouring rain. Everything was cried out of her. For the first time in a long time she felt completely empty—and clean.

THE NEXT NIGHT, unexpectedly, Candy stopped by for a beer on her way home from work. Belinda took it as a sign, God speaking to her indirectly. She hadn't believed she would ever see Candy again—but, like Grace always said, God works in mysterious ways—and here was Candy. It was like Belinda's replacement stepping in early to learn the ins and outs of the job. And Virgil was smiling like a fool.

At first Virgil didn't recognize Candy, but after Belinda nudged his memory he was smiling and saying, "What ever happened to . . . ," and little Lamar was sitting in Candy's lap, and Penny and Patsy had remembered her from Sears and were drawing her some pictures to take home with her, and all in all things went pretty well. Penny traced a yellow-haired angel from the *New Testament Coloring Book,* which Grace had given her for her birthday, and wrote *Candy* across the angel's chest. Belinda knew this was no coincidence. She nearly wept when Penny presented Candy with the drawing because she knew it was the work of God—setting her free. It made her mad. She could die now, and for the first time since her diagnosis—she was afraid.

When Candy left, promising to come to supper one Friday night soon, Virgil stood at the door watching her get in her car and drive off. Afterward, partly bewildered, partly amazed, he turned to Belinda and said, "What a pair of bazookas!"—a comment Belinda considered a religious experience.

"YOU FEEL OKAY?" Virgil asked Belinda regularly as the weeks passed. She usually said she was fine. But she had started taking lots of naps, sometimes putting all three kids in the bed with her and reading them stories out of her mother's old *Ladies' Home Journal* magazines. Everybody's favorite stories were from "Can This Marriage Be Saved?" Belinda would read both sides of it, then take a vote on whose fault it was. Most of the time it seemed to Belinda that it was the wife's fault, and Lamar always voted the same way Belinda did. Penny insisted it was the husband's fault every time. And Patsy refused to vote because she didn't want to take sides.

"Don't be reading those kids that mess," Belinda's mother said. "They ought to be listening to Bible stories or fairy tales at their age. Not marriage," she said.

"Marriage is as far-fetched as any fairy tale," Belinda said. Sometimes they watched *Donahue,* Belinda and all three kids sprawled on the sofa, eating mayonnaise and lettuce sandwiches. Whenever Phil had a panel of medical experts for his guests, Belinda changed the channel and they watched *Andy Griffith* reruns and laughed like crazy at Barney Fife making a complete fool of himself.

Belinda had small episodes of bleeding. Sometimes painful. Sleep seemed to be the best medicine. The children enjoyed Belinda's new laziness, her lying around the trailer in her pajamas until noon. Taking long afternoon naps pretending the bed was a raft and the floor was an ocean full of sharks. Playing cards for hours. Lamar was already learning his numbers.

Belinda spent some of this time telling the kids about heaven. All the same things her daddy had told her. That you can eat and drink anything you want to in heaven, because there's plenty, and it won't make you sick or fat. Food is joy—you can just gobble it up. Everybody has naturally curly hair there, you never need a comb. Nobody's skin breaks out. Nobody has crooked teeth. You get a good singing voice and automatically know the words to all the songs. And they have rock and roll in heaven—not just hymns. You can fly, stay up late, sleep on the clouds, and do anything you want to. And all the animals are tame and they have wings too, so the ponies in heaven fly. So do the big dogs and they'll let you ride them if you want to. The kids loved to hear Belinda tell about heaven—and she hoped that after she died, when Virgil said, "Your mama is in heaven," they would think about it and be glad.

But secretly Belinda was suspicious of God. She had become suspicious early on—partly because Grace had stayed so furious on his behalf for most of her life. If God was even half as angry as Grace, it would be too much to bear. For several Easters after Belinda's near drowning her mother had dressed her in crinoline, flowered hat, and white gloves, to take her to church and get her baptized. "Everytime I think that you might have drowned without ever committing your life to Jesus . . ." Grace said with tears in her eyes. But each time Belinda had panicked and started crying uncontrollably—which woke her daddy up. Hungover, he staggered into the kitchen to save Belinda from Grace, who was attempting to drag her out to the car.

Righteous and outraged, Grace and Lily went off to the Easter services while Belinda and her daddy got in the truck and drove to Greenbriar to eat barbecue. Belinda had ruined many a Sunday dress dribbling red barbecue sauce down the front of it. "You look like you been shot in the heart," her daddy said, dipping his napkin in his sweetened iced tea and smearing the stain over her chest trying to remove it. She had come home in the afternoon only to have Grace strip the new dress off her and throw it in the trash.

So it was easy for Belinda to believe God was a father and not a mother like some modern people were saying. Even so she didn't entirely trust him and had only known he was real on two occasions: when her babies had sucked her breasts and milk came out—and when she made love to Gable. Sometimes with Gable still inside her—knowing full well her daddy was watching them from above—she would look up and say thank you.

BELINDA NOTICED THAT Virgil tried to stay gone as much as he could. "Be back later," he'd say on his way out the door. And Belinda and the kids had long stopped asking where he was going. When he was home Virgil watched everything Belinda ate. "You had any vegetables today?" he'd ask. "You need to eat vegetables every day." It never occurred to him to go to the store and buy any, or bring them home and cook them.

Belinda understood Virgil. He was an easy man to understand, which is what she had loved about him in the beginning. Now sometimes she wished she didn't understand him so well. She wished she didn't know what he was thinking and how he was feeling all the time. It wore her out, but at this point it was impossible to stop understanding him. He hadn't made love to Belinda in months, not since the first mention of her spot, and it wasn't because he hadn't tried. He just couldn't seem to get his equipment going anymore no matter how Belinda tried to help him, and after a few failures he had quit trying altogether. "It's not catching," Belinda had whispered to Virgil.

"I know that."

"Then what?"

"I got too much on my mind. I can't concentrate anymore."

Belinda knew what was on Virgil's mind. It was more than the sad details of their lives, a dying wife and three kids who were going to keep on and on needing things for a long time. No job and no money. What bothered Virgil most was that he had no say in anything that happened. Nothing minded him. Maybe the kids were still young enough to think he was in charge of things. They still ran from the room when he began to shout, but they would outgrow that soon, start talking back, start asking him for big, expensive things he would be unable to get. He knew it already. Nothing minded Virgil. Not Belinda, his own wife, who refused to go to the doctor. Now, not even his body, which had practically quit on him. Once Belinda died—there wouldn't be anyone around to pretend he *was* in charge.

That's why, for the time being, when Belinda and Virgil went to bed at night sometimes she wrapped herself around him and said sweet things to him. "I'm sorry I don't feel like making love anymore."

"That's okay." Virgil lay on his back, staring at the ceiling.

"Remember that time I first saw you at the Dairy Queen, Virgil? You were the best-looking thing, eating that pineapple sundae. I said to myself, I have got to get that boy to notice me. I said that's the only boy in the world who will do."

Virgil pulled Belinda to him and hugged her tight.

VIRGIL HAD NOT got a job yet, but even without a job he had managed to get a few of the things on Belinda's funeral list, which he carried with him at all times. He had already bought her Nearly Nude panty hose and was pleased with himself over it. And he had got her two sets of fake pearl earrings since they had been on special, two for a dollar. She had tried to make him take them back because they were not at all what she had in mind. But he had kept them. He had cleared all the kids' toys out of the cedar chest and put the panty hose and the earrings in there, thinking that each item he got, he would put in the cedar chest and pretty soon Belinda would have everything she needed ready and set aside. A hope chest for the afterlife. In fact, she thought it would suit her just fine if they buried her in the cedar chest and saved the money for the casket.

ON FRIDAY MORNING Belinda drove to Huntsville to meet Gable at Madison Mall. He took off from work to help her pick out a dress. She didn't tell him it was the dress she would be buried in. Belinda had lost weight without realizing it, and after trying on a few dresses in the junior department had been sent down to the pre-teen department, where she fit perfectly into a girl's size twelve.

She settled on a pretty lavender dress with a lace collar and cuffs and a tiny bunch of fake violets at the neck. It had millions of little buttons down the back and a deep purple sash at the waist. It was as pretty as some wedding dresses Belinda had seen and since Belinda had never had a wedding dress she especially liked it. The saleslady said a bride had recently chosen that exact dress for her flower girl to wear. It cost fifty-eight dollars and Gable tried to pay for it, but Belinda wouldn't let him. She put it on layaway the way she had promised Virgil, thinking that it would probably take him the rest of his life to get it paid for, but knowing that in a pinch her mother or Lily would help pay it off.

Afterward Gable took Belinda to eat at Morrison's Cafeteria. It was her favorite restaurant and she got the fried shrimp and tartar sauce, but she couldn't eat. Gable didn't notice at first. He was telling Belinda that his wife and little boy had gone back to New Orleans—maybe for good and he didn't blame them. Gable was twenty-eight years old and had been married for what he called the ten longest years of his life. But still, he had cried when they left and promised to send his wife some money every month until she could get herself going. She was registered in a dental hygienist course in Baton Rouge. And he promised his boy, Buddy, that he would send for him in December and take him to Gatlinburg for Christmas. So now his house was empty. He lived alone and that meant he and Belinda could skip the Bare Facts and go straight to his place when they wanted to be together.

Belinda was uneasy about this news because it was something she had prayed for, but she certainly never expected God to answer her prayer. He never had in the past so she had become careless in her asking. She had been asking him for Gable pretty regularly though and thanking him for Gable too, never dreaming God would respond by sending Gable's wife off to Baton Rouge and clearing the way for them to be together like two regular people in a regular bed in a regular house.

Gable also told her that he had put in a word for Virgil at the construction company and thought there was a good chance he would get hired. This news made Belinda teary. She picked up her napkin and blew her nose.

"I want you well taken care of," Gable whispered. "That's all."

"He'll do a good job," Belinda said. "I promise. If somebody tells Virgil just exactly what to do he'll do it the best he can."

"You're not eating," Gable said, looking at the nine fried shrimp, untouched.

The truth was Belinda couldn't eat. She was feeling sick. Really sick and had been fighting it all morning because this was supposed to be such a happy occasion—all day at the mall with Gable. And tonight Candy was coming to eat supper with her and Virgil and the kids. Belinda tried to push the sickness out of her mind, but it kept coming back like ocean waves that come and go, come and go.

The waves of sickness scared her as much as the ocean that time at Gulf Shores when she was a little girl and the tide had sucked her way out over her head. The waves slapped her under again and again. She couldn't find the sky. Her daddy had swum out, grabbed her leg, and pulled her to safety. He cried and cussed while he pumped the Gulf of Mexico out of Belinda's lungs.

Her mother had stood apart from them with her eyes closed, quoting the Twenty-third Psalm. She remembered her daddy holding her up by the feet and shaking her until she vomited gallons of ocean. He pounded on her with his fists, screaming, "Breathe." Lily had run in circles around them, shrieking.

Belinda couldn't bear to waste nine Morrison's fried shrimp, partly because she didn't know if she would ever have a chance to eat them again, and partly because her daddy had raised her to eat every single bite and say it's good, whether it is or not. She had tried her best to live by that for twenty-three years.

"I can't eat it, Gable." Her face went pale. A sudden pain splashed through her. She moaned and slid low in her chair, dropping her fork which clanked against the plate.

"You okay?" Gable jumped up from his chair. She was whiter than the tablecloth and her eyes were closed. "I have to go home."

She wouldn't let Gable drive her. He wanted to take her to the emergency room but the idea upset her so much he dropped it. He literally carried her to a pay phone and held her up while she called Virgil to come get her.

"Huntsville?" Virgil shouted into the phone. "What the hell are you doing in Huntsville?"

Holding Belinda's fried shrimp in a doggy bag Gable carried Belinda out to the car as she instructed him. He bet she didn't weigh ninety pounds. He lay her down on the front seat, where she tossed her head and gripped her belly, making short, breathy shrieks. She was scaring the hell out of him.

"Baby, what's wrong? Let me get somebody."

But Belinda refused. She lay still one minute then jerked her knees up and pressed them against her chest each time a pain hit. She made terrifying noises. Gable was wild. He turned on the motor and got the air-conditioning going for her. He put the radio on the softest music he could find. He circled the car like a madman, checked the tires for flats. Opened the hood of the car and checked the oil, memorized the tag number. And in between he climbed in and out of the back seat, reached over where Belinda lay and touched her hair, touched her face, and whispered, "Sweet, sweet Baby." Sometimes she gripped his hand, pressing her fingernails into it, but her fingernails were so soft they just bent. There was no stab to them.

It took Virgil forty-five minutes to get to Huntsville. Kicker drove him. Only minutes before they arrived Belinda had insisted that Gable leave. "Virgil can't find you here," she whispered. "He'll get all upset."

Because he would do anything for Belinda, seeing her so tiny and pale, Gable obeyed her, but just long enough to pull his truck up and park it right beside her car. "I'm right here," he told her. "I'm not going to take my eyes off you until Virgil comes."

Virgil and Kicker came through the parking lot like an ambulance. Virgil was shouting Belinda's name as he ran from the truck to her parked car.

"IT'S PITIFUL WHEN you're invited to supper and you get here and have to cook it yourself," Belinda said to Candy. She was feeling better and was propped up in her bed sipping 7UP. Virgil had been frantic all afternoon. By the time Candy arrived he had finished half a bottle of gin waiting for her. Belinda heard Virgil tell Candy what a close call they had had that day. She heard him take Candy over to the cedar chest and show her its contents. She heard his choked voice and the mention of "Belinda's funeral list."

Now Candy was frying pork chops and letting Penny peel potatoes for French fries. Patsy was setting the table, asking which side the forks go on. Lamar was on his rocking horse that Belinda's mother had got at a yard sale, its springs squeaking as he bounced. Virgil was lying in his battered Naugahyde La-Z-Boy. It was folded back into the rest position, and he was drinking beer from a glass, since company was there. *Wheel of Fortune* was on. They were all playing along with Vanna and Pat. "A stretch of time," Virgil shouted. Belinda could hear them laughing. "No," Penny corrected, "too many letters."

Belinda lay in the dark bedroom at the back of the trailer. It was cool. She had a floating feeling listening to her family in the other room. They will keep on just fine, she thought. "A stitch in time saves nine!" Virgil shouted. "Daddy wins!" yelled Patsy. "Shhhhhhh," Candy said, "let Belinda sleep." Her voice had a certain music to it, mingled with the television applause and the shrieks of a woman who had a chance to win a pop-up camper if she could solve the puzzle.

Belinda leaned against the pile of pillows her family had brought to her bed. She was circled by every pillow in the house. Penny and Patsy and Lamar dragging their pillows to Belinda like three wise men bearing gifts. There were those tiny moments when Belinda would not trade her small life for any other, longer, or better life. There were those tiny moments when she felt sure.

Virgil had arranged Belinda on the pillows, arms here, legs there, head this way. Then he had turned out the light and let her sleep. She awoke to the happy noises of the children squealing as Candy pulled up into the driveway, blowing her car horn, bringing each of them a surprise, "for after supper," she said.

So this is it, Belinda thought. This is how my life will be without me. She was grateful for the sounds coming from the other room. Lamar riding his little horse nowhere. Patsy clanking dishes. Penny shouting out alphabet letters. Candy saying, "Virgil, you and the kids wash up. Supper's ready."

"Damn, fuck, shit, hell," Belinda said quietly. She had long ago checked "cuss all I want to" off her list. She often muttered every vile word she could think of—but never in front of the children—just to exercise the right to do so. Just to use up her share of cussing, to make up for all the holding back she had done all her life.

The only thing remaining on Belinda's list of "Things to Do Before I Die" was to get baptized one more time. Since that time at Gulf Shores she had been afraid to go underwater. Her mother had cried over her refusal to be baptized, saying, "Belinda, if you ever want a minute's peace you are going to have to drown yourself in the love of God."

If Belinda had to drown in somebody's love, she wished it could be Gable's. She wondered what he would do if he knew how sick she was. She wondered what he would do when she died. Who would call him? Who would explain things to him?

Virgil came stumbling down the hall to the bedroom bringing with him the warm smell of food frying. He paused in the doorway. Belinda was pale and thin, lying in her white cotton night-gown, lost in the swirl of white sheets and pillows, smudges of mascara under each eye. She smiled at him.

Virgil was awkward, afraid to enter the room. He didn't look a day over sixteen, Belinda thought. He was unusually red-faced from the gin and his hair was short and boyish. It occurred to Belinda that he had gotten a haircut in honor of Candy coming to supper. Ordinarily Belinda cut his hair with the kitchen scissors.

"You okay?" Virgil asked.

"Better."

"You scared the hell out of me."

"Me too."

"No sense in trying to talk to you about the hospital I guess."

"No."

Virgil was drunk. He propped himself against the door frame, but kept slipping away from it as if a door frame were something you could fall off of. "I feel so damn helpless," he said. He ran his hand through his hair, but his hair was too short for it to be an effective gesture. He tried to look Belinda in the eye, but it was as hard for him as it is for some people to stare straight into the sun. He squinted as though Belinda was a glare. "I wanted to be a good husband to you, I swear to God, I did. I wanted to buy you things and take you places. I don't know what all went wrong. I thought I had more time, you know."

"You did just fine, Virgil." He made her think of her daddy the way he stood in the doorway, red-eyed, not coming or going either one, just swaying, undecided. Drinking always brought out the feelings in her daddy too. When Belinda and Virgil were seventeen Belinda realized that beer, lots of beer, made Virgil romantic. He couldn't seem to get himself going without it. But after a couple of six packs he could even say "I love you." Now beer didn't work, and it took gin to get Virgil to talk. Her daddy had been the exact same way. Sometimes Belinda felt sorry for certain kinds of men.

"There is one thing, Virgil."

"What?" Virgil tried to stand up straight. "You name it and you got it."

"Don't laugh."

"I swear I won't."

"I want to get baptized."

Virgil looked at her a moment, then saluted her, slapping his heels together, spilling the drink in his hand. "One baptizing coming up. I'll get your mama to set it up at the church."

"No. Now. I want you to do it, Virgil. You and the kids. And Mama. And Candy."

"Candy?"

"You like her, don't you, Virgil?"

"Sure I do. I mean, she's all right."

"I think she likes you a lot."

"You do?"

"I know she likes you. I can tell."

Virgil's eyes filled with alcohol tears. "You deserved to be married to a doctor or a lawyer, Belinda. A man with a good credit rating. Don't think I didn't know that." Virgil shook his head to keep from getting emotional.

"Just don't hold me under too long, Virgil."

"What?"

"When you baptize me. I don't like for my head to go under."

"What am I supposed to say when I dunk you? I don't know anything religious."

"Just read something out of the Bible."

"Penny!" Virgil yelled. He stepped into the hall as Penny came running to see what he wanted.

"Is Mama okay?" she asked.

"She's fine." Virgil put his hand on Penny's shoulder to steady himself. "You run get your grandmama to come over here. Tell her we're going to have a baptizing." Penny grinned and took off running.

Virgil stumbled over to where Belinda lay. He bent over her, kissing her forehead and her shoulder. Then he scooped her up in his arms and carried her down the hall to the kitchen.

"Virgil, be careful!" Candy said. "You might drop her."

"Patsy, go run your mama a tub," Virgil said. "Get it real full." Patsy skipped down the hall to the bathroom, followed by Lamar, who ran after her dragging a pink stuffed rabbit at the end of a rope.

"What in the world?" Candy said.

"Virgil's going to baptize me," Belinda said. Virgil kept losing his balance so Belinda wrapped her arms around his neck and clung to him trying to keep him upright.

Candy stood with her arms outstretched, ready to catch them both if they tipped over. "Why don't you set her down, Virgil?" Candy said. "You're swaying."

"She ain't heavy," Virgil said. "She ain't heavy, she's my wife . . ." he sang, laughing at himself. Within minutes Penny came running into the trailer, followed by Belinda's mother, who barreled in the door, breathless. "I've waited all my life for this," she said.

"The tub's ready," Patsy shouted, pulling on Virgil's arm. "I made Mama a bubble bath."

Virgil carried Belinda down the hall to the tiny bathroom, followed by the kids and Candy and Belinda's mother, who was suddenly very quiet. Sure enough the tub was full of white suds. It looked like a tub full of cloud.

Virgil bent down on his knees. Candy rushed to his side, bracing him, helping him lower Belinda into the tub. Belinda's white nightgown billowed like a sail when it touched the water. Virgil poked at the air bubble, trying to deflate it.

"Look," Penny said. "Mama looks pregnant."

"Hush," Grace said, covering Penny's mouth with her hand.

Belinda sank into the warm, soapy water. She leaned against the edge of the white fiberglass womb and kicked her feet slightly.

"Turn off the lights," Virgil said. Candy reached over and flipped the light switch.

"Do you know what we're supposed to say, Mama?" Belinda asked.

"You ask for forgiveness, baby," Grace said, and she began shuffling through the Bible looking for a proper passage.

"Is the water too hot?" Virgil asked.

"It's fine," Belinda said.

"Then why are you crying?"

"She don't want her head to go under," Grace said. "She's always been scared of going under."

"Don't cry, Belinda," Candy said, her eyes full of tears too. She stood behind Virgil, who was squatting, leaning over the edge of the tub. Candy's knees pressed against either side of Virgil's rib cage, steadying him.

"I got you, Belinda," Virgil said. He took her face in his hands and turned her head to look at him. "I got you."

"It won't hurt, Mama," Patsy said.

Belinda closed her eyes and rested her head against Virgil's arm. The water was warm. She could smell the Lemon Joy Patsy had used to make the bubbles. She heard her mother flipping the pages of the Bible. Lamar slung the stuffed rabbit into the tub and it sank. Belinda kicked her foot lightly and the water rippled in tiny waves. She tried to remember the happiest moments of her life.

"We're not going to do a thing until you say so," Virgil whispered. "Belinda, baby, you just tell me when you're ready to go under. You just say the word."